I0520151

Jonathan Hood

in

Close the Door Behind You

by
Amurá Oñaā

Published by

UNLIMITED LLC

2018

Other books by Amurá Oñaā

The Promise
(Poem)

Amurati
Vol. 1
(50 Short Stories, 300 words or less)

Amurati - Sci Fi
Vol. II
(50 Short Stories, 300 words or less)

The Seed
(Origin of AI)

The Haven House
Co-authored with Joe Hunt

Tainted Time
(A Hundred Days in Prose)
Book I

Jonathan Hood in Close the Door Behind You is a work of fiction. The characters and names are products of the author's imagination or used fictitiously.

ISBN 978-0-578-43743-9

JONATHAN HOOD
in
CLOSE THE DOOR BEHIND YOU

Copyright © 2018 Amurá Oñaā

All rights reserved, including the right to reproduce this or portions thereof in any form.

Cover Design and Art by Amurá Oñaā

Published by Amurá Unlimited, LLC

www.amuraunlimited.com

Life can be terrifying enough
when walking through
the doors we open,
and then there are the doors
We forget to close.

Chapter 1

The apartment looked more gray than usual if gray were a flavor, there'd be no taste to the place. Was it the look or maybe the feeling? A former detective, Jonathan Hood, couldn't tell as he stepped past through the dense, creaky, fire-proof door that opened to a short, dark hallway. His achy, weary eyes ran point ahead of him and raced up over the brittle, peeling wallpaper that seemed older than he was, only to find the dark water stains radiating out from the corners of the ceiling in the room. *Damn top floor apartments,* he thought, but it was always a recurring refrain whenever he'd come through the door.

The gray, cloudy day didn't help with the place's ambiance, creating eerie, dark shadows niched between the black, ceiling-to-floor-length curtains. He switched on the light only to watch the ceiling fluorescent and the radio that played soft jazz music suddenly go dead. He went to the fuse box in the hall to shut it off and flip it back on. After several tries with the switch that appeared to be the problem, he got a little flustered and slammed the fuse box door shut, only to see it bounce back without snapping shut. "Damn fuse!" He sputtered between tight lips. The hell with it, he would find his way; he knew his dump like the back of his hand.

His only reason for returning to his flat was to get his revolver. Like his feeling about his apartment, something wasn't quite right about today. A recurring sensation, he recently began to experience a little too often the past few days, ever since he took on his last case. He had that burning sensation that somehow, somewhere, he had connected himself to a "disturbance in the force," and for some reason or another, he would have to pay for it. He had that uneasy feeling there would be payback of some kind, like that collection plate that's passed around at Sunday service. You know you got to divvy up something or have the rest of the congregation stare you down.

He found his way to a small, unstable, three-tier bookshelf, removed some books from the second shelf and grabbed his weapon hidden there, and placed it in his waist belt. He didn't like the feel, considering he unknowingly misplaced his shoulder holster two days earlier. His face hardened at the idea that things had gotten this bad, that he, a once-respected police detective, had sunken to the low-life sleaze of a private dick – Private Detective Jonathan Hood. Somehow, to him, the word "private" held a negative connotation of being "alone," which pretty much summed up his existence. While he was floundering around in his disgust, he took the gun out and tried it in a few other places, coat pocket, inside pocket, pants, only to settle with putting it back in the belt, but behind him, readjusting his strap and making sure the safety was on. The last thing he needed to do, considering the flavor of the day, was to shoot himself in the ass.

He hurriedly placed the books back, stood, and walked over to his dirty living room window to peek out on the streets. There was an indication of possible rain later in the day, but the mid-day street was quiet

He turned to go out and saw his old, worn, comfortable couch where warm memories of refreshing sleep sang sweet whispers to his tired soul. He paused and considered the appeal, shook his head, and headed back toward the door.

Before leaving, he stopped by the full-length mirror in the dim hall and took stock in his appearance in the shadow of the hallway. A good-looking, stocky, six-foot, well-built, copper-skin, black man stood there looking back at him, clothes somewhat loose due to a lack of decent meals. He tightened the knot on his black dew rag on his head that covered his short dreads and moved his hands down to his chin. "You could use a shave, ya bum!" He chuckled to himself, rubbing his hand across his scruffy beard while trying to judge the whiteness of his teeth as if he had given a damn.

Suddenly, there behind him, in the dirty, hand-smudged mirror's reflection, a shadowy, transparent apparition with sinister, glowing eyes was hovering outside of his kitchen window watching him. He quickly swerved around only to see nothing there. Out of habit, he reached for his gun in the area where his shoulder holster would typically be, only to realize it was in his back-waist belt. Upon realizing it, he nervously giggled to himself when he realized how useless it would have been against the entity he had just seen. He cautiously rushed to the kitchen window: six stories up, no way José, it had to be his imagination.

He turned back to view the full-length hall mirror from where he was standing, seeing his silhouette against the gray daylight in the window behind him, nothing. He sighed with unsure relief. He took one more glance through the window, still nothing. He slowly walked to

3

his old rusty, metal kitchen table, grabbed a bottle of whiskey out of the food cabinet, whose door had been torn off in a fight years earlier. He pulled back a worn table chair and sat, took a piece of paper out of a dirty glass on the table, and poured himself a double. He let it burn his throat, he needed to feel it hit the spot, and after another swift jig, it did. He gave one more careful look at the window, not wanting to look down at the hall mirror any time soon. He sat there, considering whether to pour himself another. He wondered if he should fix the fuse in the gray room, he decided not to. He could hear the hum of the refrigerator motor in the silence, and that was enough for now. It wasn't like he had the time to work on the switch now anyhow.

Jonathan just sat there listening to the low hum of the refrigerator, undoing his dew rag and running his hands through his short dreads, wondering if the phantoms that haunted his faltering career as a police detective were coming back to finish the job. What was he doing drinking? He made promises to himself and to those blank fading faces of people he knew, who said they cared. Really?

"So why couldn't I get rid of you?" he said, looking at the lonesome Jack Daniel's bottle sitting next to him on the table as if he expected it to shrug its shoulders. He put the cap back on it only to get up and remove it again, poured the remains into the dish-filled sink, and saved the last quarter-inch to wash his tongue that was pleading for one last taste. He turned on the coffee urn, sat, and waited, pulling the gun out and placing it on the table just to look at it while the coffee brewed.

He was already regretting dumping his whiskey down the drain. "Stupid ass motherfucker," he said, only to chuckle at the incoming memory of him spouting the very same damn words the day of his firing when he decided to remodel his captain's face with a few well-placed blows of his fists. The captain was always a prick, ever since he knew him in elementary school — an asshole who always wanted a commendation or reward for things he didn't say or didn't do.

Jonathan was just tired, tired of the bullshit protocol of assholes who couldn't manage to fit on their left shoe if they hadn't already put on the right shoe. He was tired then, like he was tired now. Drinking and drugging was a good excuse back then, but what reason did he have now? The drugs were behind him, but the boozing? Well, it was still a close, tight horse race, and he was only ahead, and if he wasn't careful, drinking could easily take the lead at any moment.

"And now this shit!" he said, thinking of the specter. "So, what's up now, Lord?" he blurted out, yelling up at the ceiling. "I'm already on the top floor; they say next stop is heaven. So, what is this new crap going on? Huh?" He got up to get his coffee. The empty silence already gave him the answer he had long come to expect – nothing. He grabbed a turned-down mug off the table, poured the hot liquid, something thicker than it should've been, and drank it black, no sugar, and it tasted as bad as the number of days it probably had been sitting there in the urn. It didn't bother him; nothing bothered him. It's been more than three years or so since Cynthia died in a tampered car. A car he was supposed to have been driving. And his life had been on a downhill spiral ever since. In sheer shock and unending depression, he was a candidate ripe for hard drugs and alcohol. When was it ever going to end?

He slammed his fist on the table, hard enough to hear the tenant below him squeal some bullshit! "Let it go!" he muttered. "Let it go! I don't need to be thinking about that crap, not today, and certainly not now! There's plenty of room for that pain later, just not now!" Was he talking to his mind, or was it the other way around? The next taste of coffee did it for him, taking his mind off that one true love in his life.

He went through his coat pocket, pulling out a few crumpled pieces of paper, accompanied by three or four crushed dollar bills. Found his worn, rolled-up notebook and, with a pencil from a cracked jar on the table, found a blank page he would mark with today's date and wrote -- Buy a fuse switch. He turned some pages back to go over some notes of a case he had started working on a few weeks ago. It was simple enough, another husband wanting to know if his wife was cheating on him or not, nothing much to it – she was, but then who wasn't these days. She was attractive enough to lure anyone looking for seduction. Hell, it could've been me in bed with her; I mean, why even hire me? It had to be evident to him, or it should've been. He pulled out his cell to check for messages, but he didn't see any.

He decided to look at pictures he had messaged his client. He then went through his email. There was an email about being paid online from his client. He had missed it. "Jonathan, you are getting sloppy, but damn, thanks for the cash; I could sure use it." He scrolled further down to see another missed email from his client dated about four days earlier; he opened it. It read, "Mr. Hood, forget what I asked of you, leave it alone. I'll be sending you money for your expenses. I'd rather not know. That's enough, thanks." "Hmm, curious," he said.

Shit, any other message I forget to read? He thought, checking to see what other clumsy act he might've made. There was nothing else but some junk mail from social groups he considered joining online. He got up from the table and replaced his gun. Check his refrigerator; the light was on – that was good enough, the fuse could wait. He went over to the fuse box and took out his cell to take a picture of the fuse switch, just in case he needed to get another one. *The damn landlord should have installed new wiring and brought this old tenement house up to specks/code years ago; that jive time mother…, should've had new switches put in, got to be some damn violation, he thought. I guess if they can play the game without doing shit, they'll play the game.*

He went to the hallway only to avoid looking at the mirror again, out of sight, out of mind, he thought. Still, he wondered about it as he slammed his door shut and put the keys in the door, and turned to go.

He could hear kids on the floors down below him playing and laughing. When he reached the level below him, there was his neighbor below him, giving him the evil eye only to timidly scurry back into his apartment as if he saw something behind or next to Jonathan. Jonathan just shrugged him off as an ol' fool.

As he got further down the stairs, he ran into the three kids looking at a video game on one of their screens.

"Why aren't you guys in school?"

"It's Saturday, Mr. Hood!"

"Oh, my bad!" he answered them. "So, it's Saturday," he mumbled to himself, wondering how in the world could it be Saturday? The damn week was flying by, he got to the door, and he checked his piece under his trench coat and went on outside.

He had been out earlier in the day, and he could have sworn it was Friday, "At forty-two years old, and my memory is going! Damn, Saturday?"

The Hawk was blowing, picking up speed and bringing with it a prickly chill that ran through his trench coat. *Damn, that was quick, it was warmer earlier in the morning, but then again, the sun was out.*

He passed by some of the staple folks in the community or "regulars," some gave him a respectful nod, while others, who he knew and who were aware of his fall from grace, purposely paid him no mind. As he walked down the avenue, there on the corner near a favorite neighborhood bar, sitting on a metal milk crate, was Blind Blinky peddling with a ragged, three-tiered paper coffee cup in hand on his sacred corner next to Jack's Bar and Grill, more bar than a grill. He wore two jackets over a dirty plaid shirt and gray jeans, a black scarf and wool cap, and a pair of used, worn black military boots that he probably picked up from a Salvation Army store or gotten from a garbage bin or another kind soul.

Jonathan reached in his pockets for a few bills before nearing him. Blinky was only a few years older than him; they had grown up in the hood together, blind or as close to it as one can get since he was a child. His birth name was Robert Conyers, but he was known on the streets as "Blinky" because that's what Robert did to get some semblance of what was going on around him. He would rapidly blink his eyes.

"Johnny, is that you?" he was one of a handful of people allowed to call him Johnny. Jonathan would generally insist on being referred to as Jonathan. He came up to Blinky and put two bills in his cup.

"Hey Blinky, how you doing?"

"Fine, and you?"

"Fine, I guess. Hey Blinky, why didn't you speak to me when I came by yesterday to park some change in your cup?"

"Nothin' personal bro, I didn't like that character with whom you were hanging! He had a bad attitude that ran for a mile and a half further than most folk."

"What are you talking about? I wasn't with anybody when I saw you yesterday!"

"Then maybe he was with you. Whoever he was, please don't bring him around again. I can't see much, but there were definitely two figures in front of me when you guys showed up."

"Did he say anything?"

"He didn't need to."

"Why didn't you say anything?"

"Man, you must be crazy. Just him standing there was enough to tell me to keep my damn mouth shut!" He said, shaking his head.

Jonathan stepped back, somewhat startled by what he had just heard. He felt an uncomfortable chill run up his spine, and it wasn't from the wind that was now going through his pockets. He began to look around him; he didn't know what for, but his mind was already running way ahead of him, trying to put the few fragmented pieces of an unrecognizable puzzle together, only to wind up with another unknown piece.

Suddenly, an unmarked car with flashing lights that came speeding up the avenue caught his eye. It made a quick U-turn when it reached near his location; two detectives he knew jumped out with their guns drawn but held them at their sides.

"Hood, up against the wall!" one of them shouted at him.

He slowly turned around, placing his hands on the bar window, only to have some of the midday patrons look at him with interest. He was pissed off and muttered to himself, "What the fuck now?"

They were two fellow detectives from his former precinct, Matthews and Samuels, former close associates from where he used to work.

Steven Matthews, a big, dark-skinned man, older of the two. He wore a dark-gray, wrinkled suit over a blue turtleneck sweater, came over, and started frisking him, and his size made him look menacing. In a deep voice that brushed past a heavy mustache, "Sorry, man, didn't want to do this, but Captain Henderson said we had to come uptown to check on you."

"What the fuck for this time? Ever since I beat the shit out of him, he's had it in for me, that dumb piece of shit!" Jonathan had a feud with Captain Mark Henderson dating back into their childhood days, ever since Mark insisted he was the best in everything when he usually wasn't, but it wasn't his place to tell these two guys about it.

"Hey!" Don Samuels, a short blond, plump dude, trying to push his chest out over his gut, but always failed and who didn't quite fit the description of a police detective, added, "You need to watch your temper, boy!"

Jonathan gave him a stern look but dismissed it, "Not when that piece of slime made a nasty remark about my dead wife, I don't! He got what was coming to him. He's just lucky I didn't kill his ass!" He caught himself when those words poured out of his mouth but decided he didn't give a shit.

"Well, I'll admit, the captain can be a real prick sometimes, especially when it comes to you, but was it worth it, breaking his nose and all?" Matthews asked.

"Yeah…," he said, taking a pause, "now that I come to think of it, yes it was!"

After Matthews frisked him, he found his revolver behind him, in his belt. "Well, what the hell is this?"

"I got a permit to carry it, and you know it!" Jonathan snapped back at him.

"No, no, I understand the gun, but where's your holster?" Matthews said, chuckling while showing Jonathan's piece to his partner.

"Oh man, now that's sad. Man, you've hit rock bottom! What happen?" Samuels asked.

"Lost my holster two days ago, now can I have my gun back?" Jonathan wasn't in the mood for any teasing he was about to endure. They might have been close when on the force, but he knew Captain Henderson was out for blood and yearning to turn his "hard life" into a "fuckin' hard life."

He reached for his gun, but Matthews moved it out of his reach. "Now, now just one minute, Hood. Hey Samuels, what was the name of the victim?"

Samuels pulled out his notepad, "Jonathan Hood, did you know of or have any dealings with a Mr. Scott Simmons?"

"Er, what?" Jonathan was taken aback by the question. First, how did they know about Scott, and what was that he-didn't-need-to-hear phrase "victim." The world around him grew numb and muffled as though someone smothered him under a thick, fluffy pillow.

"Do you want me to repeat the question?" Samuels said, looking at Jonathan, who appeared lost in thought.

"Ah, no, no, did you say victim?" His voice sounded harsh and dry, damn lousy timing on throwing that whiskey away; he could damn well use some now.

Samuels smoothly flipped one or two pages back, oh yeah. Mr. Scott Simmons, the husband of Samantha Simmons, was an accountant for Lieberman Shipping, and Exports was found dead last night, November 7th, at 7:45 pm at his place of residence.

"Ah, oh yeah, I knew him. He was my last client on a case. He had just sent me an email, paid me for my time, and just told me to forget the case. I could show you the email if you need to see it." *Why did he feel like he needed an alibi, and what kind of situation had he gotten involved in?*

Samuels was satisfied, "Hey, we go back a spell. It's all good; we'll call you in if we need to see it, okay? Man, it's hard enough skimming any worthwhile work, and then your 'skim' gets killed. Don't let this year come down hard on you; there's enough shit down here on the ground already, right Blinky?" He put a bill in Blinky's cup..

Blinky just nodded. "Amen, bro, Amen!"

While Samuels was speaking to Jonathan, Matthews had gone to the trunk of his car and pulled out a used, worn leather holster, put Jonathan's revolver in it, made sure it was snug, and brought them back to Jonathan. "Here, man, until you get another holster again. And yo, straighten up, you know you do look like a worn piece of dried shit!" he said, smiling.

"Your mama!" Jonathan yelled back at him as Matthews and Samuels returned to their car. "Hey, I owe you one, Matthews," he added, putting on the shoulder holster.

Matthews waved him off, "You owe me more than one, Chump!" Both he and Samuels got back in and drove off laughing. Matthews knew Captain Henderson wanted them to bring him in; he just didn't have the heart and wouldn't admit it cause Jonathan was still "family." He had to convince Samuels, who was usually a lapdog for Henderson. However, both he and Samuels could tell that Hood was just at a loss for what happened to Mr. Simmons as they were. And they had yet to say to him the condition of the body; it was a ritualistic death with unknown symbols all around his body, as well as markings on Jonathan Hood's business card along with a few other business cards found next to Simmons.

"Blinky, I need a quick drink. Want to join me at Jack's Bar? I'm buying." He said, helping a shaky Blinky to his feet. He could tell Blinky had been sitting a little too long on his crate that held a bunch of old newspapers rubber banded to the top for a cushion; he handed him his cane.

"Hell, Johnny, I thought you gave up drinking?"

"So, did I, but there's always tomorrow, you coming or not?"

"Hell, who am I to say no?" he said, putting his cups with his change in his fabric bag draped across his shoulder.

When they entered the bar, most of the twelve or so patrons sitting around gave Blinky a warm welcome, with only a few of them offering a nod or a raised glass to Jonathan. The lighting in the bar was dim. It had candles on tables and strings of small holiday lights strung across the ceiling and over the bar area. Most of the lighting came in through the windows.

"I see they treat you pretty much like the rest of us, now that you ain't part of the boy's club anymore, eh ex-Detective Hood!" said one of the sneering patrons who saw him padded down through the window.

Jonathan wanted to say something back.

"Let it go, Johnny!" said Blinky, "Get me a seat, and I got a taste for a Black Russian, haven't had one since God knows when."

"No problem Blinky." He sat Blinky down and went to the bar to get his order, all the time giving that patron a hard look as he walked on over to the bar.

He turned to Larry, the bartender, gave him a nod of greeting, and ordered a Black Russian and a shot of whiskey. He returned to his table, sending the same guy a challenging look, enough to make the man finish his drink, get up, and leave. Hood had a respected reputation when he was on the force, but another dangerously stubborn, hot-tempered side to him that ran the streets and only spoken of in safe places.

Blinky thanked him and nursed his drink after Jonathan guided his hand to the glass; meanwhile, Jonathan put his glass down on the table. He sat, and his eyes followed the guy out, and then he turned his gaze on his shot glass in front of him. He was more interested in its look rather than its taste for now.

"Something's not right, Blinky."

"A lot of things aren't right; which one are you talking about this time?"

"Matthews, he didn't say much, and as friendly as he tried to make things look, he was holding something back; there's something he couldn't say in front of Samuels."

"Why? What was it he didn't say?"

"I think he wanted to tell me more about the case concerning my client, Mr. Simmons, but Samuels, though a nice guy, has a bad habit of bringing up shit in front of the captain. I better make some plans to contact Matthews and see what's up." He never looked up when he spoke to Blinky, just kept staring at the whiskey glass in front of him.

"Still miss her, don't you, buddy?"

He didn't even have to say who. Jonathan knew who automatically, "Cindy, yeah, you know I do. Sometimes we would sit at that table in the corner over there and small-talk our lives away; we'd hold hands and nose-snuggle like young folks, too stupid to see the train down the tracks, lights blaring and horn snarling loud as hell amid our blissful innocence. Yeah, I miss her, probably always will. Lord knows you can't say I didn't love her enough!" He grabbed hold of the shot glass and looked out through the window onto the street, trying his best to control the tears collecting in his eyes. "There's no asking why anymore; the only person's time I'm wasting is my own." He chugged down his drink.

15

"Hope you don't mind my two cents, but for a blind man, she was a hell of a good-lookin' woman!"

Jonathan busted out laughing, "Don't mind at all!"

Blinky was glad just to put a smile on Jonathan's face.

Jonathan reached to get his ringing cell phone, waited for a few rings, "Matthews, I was wondering if we could find a place to talk? Later on today? Sure, Westside, 145th? No problem, I'll see you in about two hours. Lose the kid, would you? Thanks." He put his cell away.

"You know Blinky, you and I don't hang out the way we used to do when we were kids."

"Ah, if you mean you don't play those ol' damn 'tricks-on-the-blind kid' shit. I'd rather we didn't hang."

Jonathan chuckled at the thought of some of the pranks he and his buddies played on Blinky, "Oh yeah, sorry 'bout that. You were such a good straight-man back in those days. It was just too hard to resist. I'm sorry, buddy."

"Yeah, well it hasn't been the first time you've said sorry to me."

"Oh yeah, right!" They both chuckled.

"Honestly, Blinky, I've never asked you. How well do you see?"

"A pretty good question, I guess. Most folks wouldn't bother to ask. Shimmering darkness, if there is such a description, one of light over shadow and the other being of shadow over light. Many of the things I saw when I was a child, my Mama would say was my imagination. I had a habit of calling some of the things

I saw 'crossovers,' to help me deal with them being different, but maybe my Mama was right; it was all in my head."

"Crossovers?" Jonathan asked.

"Yeah, I guess when I was a kid, I thought I could see things slip into view, like coming from some unknown place. Mama called me her crazy little peanut."

"That guy you saw with me yesterday, ah, would you say, I can't believe I'm asking you this, ah, would you say he was a 'crossover'?

"Man, you kidding me, right? My Mama talked me out of that nonsense; I don't believe in that stuff anymore, nor should you. Do you want the world to start calling you crazy? Let me guess; you lost your job, now you're about to lose your mind?"

He got a little too loud for Jonathan, as he caught the attention of a few folks in the place. He was moving a little outside Jonathan's comfort zone. "Shush, keep it down, will you? I'm just asking if there was anything about him, anything your blind little ass might've noticed?"

"Oh man, that hurt, but I will tell you this much," Blinky said.

"What?"

"He was shadow over light! But honestly, Jonathan, it's not for me to decipher its meaning. Talk to Cindy every once in a while, don't mourn her, talk to her, cause sometimes I get the impression she's walking beside you sometimes. There are a lot of folks out there we don't talk to anymore, walking amongst us who would like us to remember them the way we knew them – as friends, like lovers, like family. We be focusing on the past, thinking they're gone when their spirits are right with us." He raised the rest of his Black Russian toward the ceiling in toast fashion, "Right, Mama? Love you."

Jonathan pushed his seat back, "Well, um, thanks for the insight. I got a few things to do before I meet up with Matthews. Can I help you back to your spot?"

"Nah, man, I got it. This place and that corner outside are the closest things to being home. Man, thanks for the drink; now I got to go take a whiz."

Jonathan helped him up and watched Blinky work his way through the tables and seating arrangement with no problem. He didn't notice the bracelet Blinky slipped into his inside pocket. Damn, he walks better than I do, he thought, feeling the rush and sway from standing too fast after his drink. What Jonathan didn't see was Blinky reaching in his bag on the way to the bathroom, pulling out a charmed, bone necklace and placing it around his neck, and muttering a few well-chosen prayers to himself.

Meanwhile, Jonathan pulled out his phone and went through a few pictures of his wife Cynthia, one of them was a copy of an old photograph of them at that table in the corner. He smiled, "So you're still with me, sweet lady?" He could imagine her saying, "What you think?" or was it his imagination? He put the cell away retreated to the avenue, thinking more fondly of her than he had done in a long time. There was a lot more to Blinky than he could've imagined, a lot more insight or "sight," for that matter, than he ever gave him credit. As he strolled down the avenue, he began to wonder just how many unknown gifted people were out there, those told to forget their gifts for fear of the views and opinions of a hostile society.

He checked his shoulder holster and fell in sync with the feel, a sensation that, oddly enough, provided him comfort. The idea that someone would kill Scott Simmons didn't make any sense to him; he seemed to be a decent enough guy from all appearances, a man who had merely lost his touch to a woman with whom he had wanted to stay in touch.

Jonathan parked his butt against the wall of a tenement building along the way down to 145th street. He pulled out his phone to see if there was anything in the emails from Mr. Simmons that might have given some indication that there was something wrong or missing, something that might give him a clue as to what the hell was going on. Then in an email written less than a month ago, he caught sight of the phrase "I don't know who or what she's gotten herself into, but could you find out? Something's not right, I can feel it in my bones if you'll pardon the expression!"

Maybe it was less of a "who" and more of a "what." He had confirmed pictures of a definite someone, but only to show Simmons she was seeing someone. Since Simmons seemed to want proof that she was having an affair, Jonathan thought giving him evidence would be the end. He would post his pictures, get his pay, and go on about his business. Now Jonathan was beginning to realize that maybe as a detective, Jonathan was a little sloppy with the case, but no, it was your basic "one plus one equals two" scenario. He made a few notes in his pad and finished up. Jonathan looked up only to see a stranger across the avenue, standing there looking at him. A woman was walking by; maybe he was watching her, nope, she had passed, but he still had his eyes set on Jonathan.

Jonathan stood up off the wall, looked away, and offered a half-hearted nod before continually to 145th. Maybe the guy was somebody he knew, and he had just forgotten, or perhaps it was another foot soldier sent out by Captain Henderson to keep an eye on him; either way, a shallow "good-bye" wave should be enough to rid himself of this guy. The thought of Captain Henderson made him spit and cuss under his breath. He had to meet Matthews.

Chapter 2

Jonathan made his way up the hill on 145th and down the hill toward Riverside Avenue. He probably could have gone back to get his ride. Still, there was something about walking. The pacing of each step allowed him to hold on to an idea. And turn it over and over for better scrutiny. By the time he got there, the day had begun to clear up, becoming warmer as the sun finally broke through the clouds. Jonathan kept looking up and down the street, trying to guess where Matthews might've parked. He reached in his coat pocket to get his phone when he started to hear a car horn blaring park side, up the block near 146th. It was Matthews.

When he reached Matthews, he got in on the passenger side.

"How's the holster holding up?" Matthews asked.

"It's fine so far, a lot better having my gun there than in the back over my ass!"

Matthews grinned, pulled out a report envelope, and handed it to Jonathan, saying, "Got to get it back before someone notices it's missing or I'm missing. Lord knows, if Henderson is watching you, he's probably watching everyone close to you, including my ass."

Johnathan put on some plastic gloves before opening the envelope and skimmed over the report concentrating more on the glossies showing the condition of Scott Simmons' naked, tied-up body and symbolic markings all along the walls of his apartment. He took out his cell and asked Matthews, "Do you mind?" Indicating he wanted to take some shots.

"The only time I saw you happened earlier today with Samuels, other than a call, I never saw you, but if your dumb ass comes across anything, I got first dibs."

Jonathan nodded. It took him short work to copy the photos and some of the report papers onto his cell phone: he closed the envelope and handed it back to Matthews while stepping outside of the car. He turned and leaned in through the open window. "Anything you can leak?"

"Only the usual, there were five cards with markings, as you saw in the photos, yours is among them. We're checking the other people involved; those on the marked cards."

As Jonathan pulled back from Matthews' car, a heavy branch broke off and fell, missing him by less than an inch as some smaller branches nearly scratched his face. It took out Matthews' right-side mirror, denting the door frame and fracturing his windshield. The sound of the crash startled them both, causing Jonathan to jump further back while looking up only to catch the tail-end wisp of a shadow vanishing above him.

"What the fuck?' Jonathan yelled, frantically trying to clear some of the dust and debris from around his eyes. "Damn, that branch could've broken my back!"

"Shit, the last thing I need to explain to Captain Henderson is how did I wind up driving your ass to a hospital? Look at this mess! Get the hell out of the way and let me take some pictures of the damage for my insurance company when I file a report." Matthews barked.

After taking a few shots of the damage and collecting the broken side mirror lying on the curb, Matthews huffed and angrily stomped back around to the driver's side of his car. "Now, let me get the hell out of here before something else goes wrong." One could see he was pissed way past his naturally calm demeanor. He revved his motor, "Jonathan, keep your head above water. Stay sharp, my brother; seems like you and shit happening go together!"

"Hey Steve, before you go," he quickly shouted to Matthews, "Does Henderson have anyone following me?"

"The Cap? Nah, I don't think so, but with a man like him, anything is possible."

Jonathan had just wanted any chance info on the guy he saw earlier, the one who was staring at him on the avenue previously as the thought of him flashed in his mind's eye. He watched Matthews pull off as he continued brushing the dust from his dreads and coat. He shook himself like a mutt shaking off rainwater. Three kids passing by gave him the full birth this "wacko" needed, comparing him to the large branch next to him, drawing their own conclusions as to what might've happened.

He walked down park side, and every so often, he'd look back to take a glimpse and gauge the size of the branch from a distance. The further he got from it, the more he realized just how close a brush with death he came or, at the very least, serious injury.

"What else can wrong today?" he said to himself.

A few seconds passed when a sharp level of high anxiety made his body shudder as though someone had walked over his grave. Jonathan needed to get a hold of himself and the events of the day. He didn't need to have things get away from him like some mad dogs off the leash only to come back at some point and bite him in the ass.

He walked south for a few blocks until he found an empty park bench free from any nearby over-hanging branches. He sat down, facing out onto the Hudson River, and figured he'd use the time to go over the recent pictures in his phone.

He studied how the Simmons' body was tied, partly nude with eyes removed and his tongue purposely extended from his mouth. It looked like some ritual ceremony was going on. There were strange unearthly-type symbols on the floor and wall around him drawn in Simmons' blood, as well as on his body.

He zoomed in on the shot of the five business cards, his among them, took out his notebook, and jotted down the names and addresses. He didn't want to get in the way of the police investigation, so he had to be careful in his approach to the case. There was Ms. Judith Andrew, a sculptress or 3-D modeler into art restoration/replication; a Dr. Roy Peters, a chiropractor; a Capt. Joseph Walker, a cargo shipping company, and a Mr. Francisco Sierra, proprietor of an antique shop.

There was nothing unusual about the group of individuals, nothing out of the ordinary, at least for now. Were the business cards chosen at random? Were they the only cards he happened to have on him at the time, or was there something more and these five selected with a purpose in mind? The question that kept coming to the surface as he went over the photos on his phone was, are these people in any way connected to Simmons' wife Samantha and her affair, and if so, why wasn't she harmed? Was she involved? She didn't seem like the type to be into rituals, just a fun-loving, lonely housewife looking for a bit of fun and excitement,

What about the man she was seeing, but who, for there were three men? He thought about how he only sent photos of her affair with one of the men; he didn't want to crush his client's heart. He'd figured one was enough for him to send to his client, enough to start whatever it was he intended to begin with his wife.

Jonathan quietly sat in deep thought with his eyes hypnotically fixed on the dancing waves of the Hudson River. He knew that soon, he would need to speak to Samantha, Scott's wife.

He knew he couldn't speak to her while she was currently under investigation unless he could figure out how to go about it differently. He didn't want to pose as a police detective; he was under enough trouble as it was already. Approaching her as a private eye working for her husband was an even worst idea. He would need to keep out of the line of sight of anyone from his former precinct and any other officer on the force who might know him from elsewhere.

He was fidgeting with one strand of his dreads when the thought popped into his head. *Dreads have got to go. Shave the beard stubs down to a goatee.*

It was time to change his look, Jonathan knew it wouldn't make that much of a difference, but if it made someone hesitate or think twice for more than a few seconds, it was an advantage he might be able to use to his benefit. He thought he might even have a chance of throwing that specter off his tail. Quietly, he started to laugh at himself for considering the idea.

He slowly got up and stretched, preparing himself for the walk back up 145th St. In his mind; he played with the thought of what type of haircut he should get. He finally settled on going bald because no one other than Blinky and a few others from the old neighborhood, who knew him in his youth, had ever seen him bald. His thoughts came to rest on Cynthia, who fell in love with him, a young man with long dreadlocks, and who asked him to grow them again, should he ever leave the force. He shook his head, "The damn sacrifices I make! Sorry baby."

When he reached Matt's Barber Shop, he looked through the window to gauge the number of customers and get a quick headcount; he wasn't in the mood for waiting for a barber. He would use it as a sign to get or not get his hair cut, but there, sitting in an empty chair, mid-way in, his ol' time barber Bat Matt, nicknamed after some 50's TV western. He hadn't seen him in years, and he was beginning to feel self-conscious as why it took him this long to stop by. Matt relaxed in the seat, carefully going over some article in a newspaper nearly covering up his dark-skinned, white-haired, heavy-face self. He appeared to grow worried as he read the article in front of him, and it looked like the next page he'd turn would reveal new wrinkles to the seventy-six-year-old neighborhood icon that everybody knew.

Jonathan opened the door only to hear that ol' familiar chime announcing a customer; it reminded him of days of his youth.

"Hey, Bat, Matt!" He said as he came in.

Matt folded the paper and comically adjusted his rims, "Jonathan, is that you? Well, as I live and breathe!" After putting the paper down as Jonathan walked in, his eyes lit up, making him look about six or seven years younger. He started to get up, but Jonathan motioned him to stay seated as he went over to greet the elder. Bat Matt continued, "Well, I'll be damned if I'm not already, Jonathan. God bless. Good to see you!"

"Eh, how're you doing, Matt? Long-time no see."

"Long time, my ass!" Bat Matt added, gingerly getting up from the chair with his black and ivory cane to give Jonathan a warm hug. He then just as quickly turned around to brush the chair off and swiveled it toward Jonathan, assuming he came in for a cut, still nimble as ever Jonathan thought. "Take a seat. Man, where have you been?"

"Out and about."

"What, you can't come by and say hi? Grown too big for your britches?"

"Nah, it's not you, just doing the ostrich thing, with my head up my ass the last few years."

"Yeah, I guess I can relate to that, but I have seen neither hide nor hair of you since Cindy's funeral." Jonathan hung up his coat and sat as Matt draped him. "Word has it you got fired, but if you don't want to wag that tail, I can understand."

"Hell, I appreciate your concern, and please accept my apologies, but enough about me. How have you been doing? Bat Matt, you lookin' good though, almost younger than when I saw you last. What's your secret?"

"It's cause he's leaving them young women alone and keepin' hold of his seed," remarked one of the older

27

gents putting on his coat to leave, having overheard their conversation.

"Shut your yap, Lenny!" snapped Matt, chuckling, along with others in the shop.

Jonathan could see Lenny chuckling as he headed out, waving to him and shooing Matt off as he went, "Take it easy, lover boy!" leaving others to continue laughing.

"Hmph," muttered Matt returning his attention to Jonathan, "So what you want done?"

"Take it all off," he hesitated a second, then confirmed it, "Yeah, take it off."

"If I remember correctly the last time I cut your dreads was when you were deciding to go into law enforcement. Correct me if I'm wrong."

"Nah, that's about right, but it wasn't a bald cut, just a decent afro cut; this time, I want it all off and clean enough of my face to leave a goatee."

Jonathan closed his eyes and relaxed back in the chair while the old man worked his face and head with talented fingers. After the workout, out came the electric shears, and dreads started to rain onto the shop floor. Jonathan didn't want to look in the mirror across from him; he just wanted to enjoy the touch of someone massaging his scalp along with the feel of the warm, steaming towel and shave cream. He just closed his eyes; it was a moment for fonder memories of more carefree times.

Bat Matt worked his magic on Jonathan, finishing up with his perfected elixirs of scented fragrances. As he was nearing completion and seeing Jonathan waking from his rest, he padded him on the shoulder and brought up the newspaper he had been reading when Jonathan first came into the shop.

"Jonathan, you know anything about this?" he asked, showing him the paper. The headline read: "Accountant Found Brutally Murdered!" His client's face was in the smaller photo box off to the side, but he didn't want Matt to know he knew anything about it.

He took the paper from Matt to take a closer look; Matt began powdering Jonathan's neck area. "Wow, no, no, I don't. Why you ask?"

"I know his older brother Ray, Raymond Simmons; he owns the ol' ophthalmologist shop down on Seventh Ave., Adam Clayton Powell Jr. Boulevard around the corner from here. I can only imagine how he must be taking his brother's death. That's rough, man, downright sickening."

"Yeah, I can only imagine." Jonathan handed back the paper to Matt.

"I hear tell you're a P.I. these days, is that true?"

"Yeah, nothing glamorous, just a job."

"You ever think about leaving New York?"

"Nah, not really; not yet anyway. You know how hard it is to get away from this magnet of a city."

Jonathan got up and stepped forward to the wall mirror to examine his cut. "Nice job, Matt, nice job."

"You're damn lucky you got a well-shaped head; some folks find out their skulls look a mess after that kind of cut. I mean, it's not like I can pick up their hair and paste it back on their head." He said, chuckling and shaking his head, sweeping up Jonathan's hair.

Jonathan stood in front of the mirror, admiring his new look, realizing the work he would have to put in to keep it up. Then he started thinking, *What are the odds I would come to Matt's Barber Shop, not to have been here in years, only to find out my client's older brother is a regular customer here? Weird.*

Jonathan gave Matt his due along with a generous tip and grabbed his coat off the rack. Curious, he felt something in the vicinity of his coat's inside pocket. He reached inside to see what it was. It was a prayer bracelet, now who would put a prayer bracelet in his jacket, then it came to him – Blinky!

"What the f...!" There was more to Blinky than he wanted folks to know. He stood there, shaking his head.

"What's that you got in your hand?" Matt questioned.

"Err, nothin', nothin' really, just a gift from an old friend. He put it back in his pocket. He'd talk to Blinky about it later when he saw him. Right now, he needed to go and see if he could meet this Raymond Simmons, Scott's brother, according to Matt. He would scamper over to Seventh Avenue.

He looked at his watch and realized it might be too late, for darkness was now camped well in the hood and wouldn't be leaving for a while. He had decided he would visit Ray tomorrow but shrugged off the idea and decided to at least take a look at the place where Matt's brother worked, as he needed to familiarize himself with its location. He noticed Matt had hats for sale on another rack by the door. He grabbed a wool cap and handed Matt a five-bill. Jonathan could already feel the breeze coming through the door and wrapping around his skin-tight head as a customer entered through the door. Without a doubt, it was something he hadn't felt in a long while.

He went out with a compliment to Matt on a job well done. He's still got the "touch," he thought as he hurried down toward Seventh. He turned the corner just in time to see someone about a block and a half away, sending down the store gate by remote.

Jonathan quickstepped it down to the store, hoping to get there before the man left.

"Excuse, excuse me, sir? Are you Raymond Simmons?

"Er, yes I am, but I don't have time to talk to you; I have personal business to attend to."

"Yes, if it involves the death of your brother, you have my condolences."

"What, you knew my brother, Scott?" He looked surprised, if not quite sure how to react to this stranger in front of him.

Jonathan put his hand in his coat to retrieve his business card.

Mr. Simmons took a few anxious steps back in anticipation of possible harm.

As Jonathan handed his business card, he said, "I was working a case for Scott."

Mr. Simmons regained a relaxed composure, "Jonathan Hood? Let me guess, following around that 'piece of shit' he called a wife?"

Now it was Jonathan's turn to be taken a little aback by the statement. "So. you knew?"

"Everyone close to Scott knew; she probably knew everyone knew too. She didn't give a shit! Listen, I'd like to talk, but I got to get going.

"Eh, I need to ask you a quick question. I'd like to talk to Samantha about the case, but not as her husband's P.I., but rather as yours."

"Sorry, I can't afford a P.I.; let the cops handle it."

"It's pro bono, no charge. I am concerned with what happened to Scott and why." *Maybe even more than you,* he thought to himself.

"Really? And why is that?"

"Because something's not right, and I feel it may impact the lives of some other people to whom your brother may have known."

"Pro bono, you say?"

"Yeah," Jonathan nodded.

"Alright," he turned to go.

"One more quick favor," Jonathan leaked out.

"What?" he sounded like he was getting slightly irritated.

"Don't let any of our New York Finest know I'm on the case."

"What are you afraid of?"

"Eh, nothing, it's just a case of professional courtesy so that we won't step on each other's toes. They got their way of doing things; I got mine."

Simmons looked at the business card again to ensure he got the name right, "Sure, Jonathan, whatever. A pleasure to meet you. I'm Raymond. Let me know what you find out." Raymond shook his hand and waved him off as he walked toward his car.

Jonathan turned around, feeling pumped that things had worked out for him. He gave a kiss up to heaven, thanking the Lord and Cindy. He smiled and retraced his steps back to Bat Matt's Barber Shop, then weaved his way up the avenue and home.

He stopped at a hardware store along the way and picked up the fuse switch he needed in case his jive-time super would complain he was out of them. He would catch Blinky tomorrow.

Chapter 3

Tossing and turning, unable to fight back, unable to flee, an unworldly creature held him down in a death grip. It relished the chance of pinning him to the forest floor while its wicked tongue licked the sides of his sweating face as he squirmed in a futile attempt to free himself. Above him, lightning fractured the night sky at a maddening pace, rumbling the earth beneath him.

In an instant, he found himself hovering above his tormented form with a burning jungle all around him. He could see below him his body still struggling. The creature's head jolted upward as if it sensed his presence had changed. It snarled, leaping up at him, no longer caring for the body it was shredding to pieces. It wanted him.

He flew through the forest brush to escape the horrid growls and snapping teeth just behind him. The saliva it spewed was akin to hot molten lava, burning him as he fled. He raced across the jungle floor, unable to gain the height he felt he should've been able to get while having the sensation of flight.

The bushes with thorns painfully scratched and tore at his face and upper torso as he fled, even with the sensation of transparency. He felt an ever-creeping surge of terror crawl up his spine when just as quickly, he found himself several hundred feet before a square-like, glowing portal located on the jungle floor, discharging sparks and spurring molten debris. Thrown aside was one of the massive stone doors that must have covered the entrance, while another door, with an enormous guardian statue, was sealed closed. He realized the opened portal should have been concealed as well, only it wasn't.

From behind him, the jungle shook with the beast's rage as the menacing creature cried out in anger. Suddenly the portal appears far away from him. The monster, beast, or whatever it was, was gaining on him as he felt himself being drawn or instead pulled toward the opening, only to hear horrid sounds discharging out from its depths. He found himself unable to tear himself away as it dragged him closer and closer. Suddenly something grabbed him by the nape of his neck and yanked him into the light. It was his wife, Cindy. She peered into his eyes, kissed him, and then slapped the hell out of him.

He woke up in a cold sweat, peering into the darkness of his room, expecting to find something or someone there in the place with him. The sheet beneath him was soaking wet from his perspiration. Jonathan pushed himself up, exhausted and weary, only to sit on the edge of his bed, pulling the blankets over him as he felt a chill. "It's November; what the hell? That was weird, and what was that thing chasing me? It looked a mix of half-wolf, half-bear, part reptile with some other unknown hideous creature. Shit! That was draining; I feel exhausted."

He got up in a daze and went to look out the window as if looking for answers to his nightmare. There was nothing, nothing but the endless darkness of the night to offer him a response. He turned on the bedside lamp and went to get himself a small glass of water, dragging the covers that he had wrapped himself in behind him. He looked at the clock; it was only 3:04 am. "Damn, that dream seemed as long as hell itself, but it's only a little after three."

He went back to his bed, ripped off the wet sheet, and grabbed another one from the drawer and threw it on, switched off the lamp, turned his pillow over, and climbed back into bed. His mind had difficulty pushing the dream out of his head. He laid there searching the darkness of the room as though he wasn't sure if he was alone. As his eyes grew accustomed to the dark, his eyes came to rest on his weapon in his holster slung over a chair in a corner. It took him a while, but sleep finally reclaimed him with little to no repercussions from the frightening dream.

The morning found him rested but thinking about Cindy and how she came to his rescue by slapping his ass back into the waking world. It was a little after nine in the morning, and the sunlight was breaking through the shades, lighting up his room only to highlight the level of its lack of color; still, at least the day was brighter than yesterday.

He decided to wear a dark blue suit with a gray turtleneck sweater. He laid the clothes out on the bed while he went to pour himself some bran flakes with some cranberry juice and coffee. Walking into the kitchen now only caused him to feel nervous about taking a glance at the hallway mirror and the kitchen window. After finishing up his breakfast, his cell phone rang. It was Matthews.

He answered, "Matthews, what's up? Everything okay?"

"Hey Jonathan, I thought I'd just let you know that Syd Barnes was released from prison yesterday evening on a technicality."

"Get the hell out of here; that's not possible! We had him dead to rights; there's no way!"

"Well, thanks to the piss-ass-shitty record of the prosecutor, someone fucked up again!"

"You and I and the whole damn department know it was probably his goons who killed my partner Chris. That motherfucker!" What he didn't tell Matthews were his suspicions that it was probably the same goons responsible for the death of his wife, Cindy.

"I know you're pissed, Jonathan; I'm just calling you to let you know you need to keep your head down and stay alert. Your death was a promise he made to you in open court. Make sure he doesn't keep it!"

"Thanks for the heads-up. I appreciate it; like things ain't bad enough already."

"What you mean by that?"

"Eh, nothing, I was just thinking out loud!"

"Okay, bud, just watch your back."

"Sure, no problem. Thanks, Matthews." He hung up.

So, Syd Barnes is back on the streets. Too many coincidences are taking place around the same time. Jonathan quickly put together a scenario of Syd having difficulty trying to reclaim his seat on the throne, but he realized he did have loyal followers in his organization. How many or how few were still alive? Hood didn't

37

know. There was no way of telling, for Jonathan had been out of the loop for the last few years and he didn't give a damn about who was now in charge of Barnes' drug empire. However, Jonathan just realized that there was a target on his back in more ways than one. He hoped Syd would take his sweet time before going up against him, after all, his threats were a public record.

He finished up his meal and went into the bedroom to finish dressing; he had a few stylish hats he hadn't worn in years. He picked the dark gray one, one of Cindy's favorites. He looked good, and he knew it, very much like his younger days.

He grabbed his holster, some personal stuff, and his car keys. He needed his ride. He preferred walking to riding; there was something about the feel of the rhythm he always got from walking the beat and how it keenly blended in with the rhythm of each neighborhood, but Jonathan needed his wheels to make some of the stops he needed to make. First on his list was to visit Mrs. Samantha Simmons, Scott Simmons' wife, and have a short chat with her, and then he would go over to the east side and talk to Mr. Francisco Sierra, the proprietor and antique dealer.

He wrapped his trench coat over his shoulder; he would put it on as he went down the stairs. He loved his trench coat; it reminded him of the early western heroes of his childhood. As he walked down the street, a few questionable looks followed him; his new look was doing its job, putting him out of context with most of the neighborhood folks who were familiar with him. They thought they knew him; they couldn't place him, so most didn't know whether to nod out of acquaintance or just out of respect for the "gentleman" walking down the street.

He picked up a newspaper along the way, and by the time he reached Blinky's spot, Blinky had a broad smile on his face. "Well, I'll be damn if it ain't 'Retroman,' famed superhero, out from the distant past, looking to save us all in the future! I haven't seen that look in ages." He laughed in delight at seeing Jonathan, his eyes fluttering like the wings of a hummingbird.

Jonathan started to reach in his inside pocket for the beads, but Blinky caught on too quick.

He raised his hand and turned away, his body language speaking volumes, "No, no thank you, things given from the heart belong to the heart it's given to."

Jonathan changed his tune, "You're something else, Blinky. I just wanted to tell you thanks."

"Sure, you did, and that I'm beautiful as well." They both laughed.

Jonathan looked at him and asked, "Can you set aside some time on your busy schedule to discuss this and your relationship to this – stuff?"

"For you? Anything, but right now, I'm guessing by the new look that you have places to go and people to see," Blinky answered.

"You're right there, bud," he said, placing two bills in his cup and turning the corner to get to his ride further down the block. "Catch you later."

"Stay safe," Blinky threw back at him.

He took his "silver bullet" downtown on the west side to the Simmons' address, but as he neared the place on 84th street, he saw a patrol car parked on the corner. He found a parking space two blocks further down where he could pull over. He slid in and opened his newspaper, pretending to be reading as he adjusted his rear-view mirror to monitor the cop car behind him.

After a while, a third policeman came up the block and got in, and they drove off. Jonathan got out, paid the meter, and walked back uptown to Simmons' block and walked down. He liked the way the sunlight hit the limestone brick of the brownstones lined up down the street. He reached the address and rang the doorbell. A tall, dark-skin beauty came to the door and pushed the curtain aside from the front glass door.

She put the chain on before unlocking and opening the door. "Yes?"

Jonathan passed her his card and told her that Raymond, Scott's brother, had asked him to look into the case involving Scott's death.

"What, that cheap, tightwad actually decided to pay for something?" She said, somewhat disbelieving it.

Jonathan didn't answer her. He just raised his eyebrows and shrugged his shoulders.

She opened the door to let him in; she had an erotic way of walking that pulled him down the hallway behind her. Yeah, he thought, *she could have any man she wanted, even me for that matter, she's certainly has a sweet --*

She swerved her head around as if she knew what he was thinking and to check if he was still under her spell. She pointed to a room further down the hall with police tape closing it off from public access. "I found his body in that room in the back," she said.

Jonathan immediately concluded that something was wrong with this picture. What was she still doing here? In fact, why did he even think she'd be here in the first place? He was slipping. The whole house should've been cordoned off, sealed. He looked behind him and noticed the inside door to the residence revealed a broken seal. How did he miss it? What could she have said to authorities that would've allowed her to come back or stay?

"Err, I hope you don't mind me asking, but why are you still here in the house alone with such a recent crime scene?"

He turned back around only to see her inches away from his face staring at him. A shroud of darkness appeared to scroll down over her features like a stage curtain, her eyes went blank, and her voice dropped a few octaves. It came out hoarse deep and angry, "Why the same reason you're here, Jonathan!"

He was thrown off guard by her abrupt change. Her right fist caught him with what felt like a massive blow to his chest, flinging him back down the hall only to land hard on his back. He laid there for what seemed like an eternity, heaving and trying to recapture the breath that she knocked out of him, but before he could recover, she or it was on top of him, ready to dice his face. She or it grabbed him by his trench coat only to cause the bracelet to fall out. Once it caught sight of it, it roared mournfully, backing away. Whatever it was, it flew out of her, causing her to fall back limp on the floor. He felt something rush over him and smash through the glass of the inside door. It shook the outside door as it headed out onto the street.

He finally got up and helped Samantha to her feet. She, like him, was groggy; they struggled toward a couch in the living room and collapsed on it. After a few minutes, he got up to pour her and himself a glass of water. Her head was beginning to clear, but she didn't have any idea what was going on.

"Samantha, do you have any place to go, family member or a friend?" He realized he was talking to her as though she was someone he knew. He was only asking her because he was concerned for her safety, but still, there was something about the incident that bonded him to her, something he didn't yet understand.

In a drugged-like fashion, she nodded. "Gloria, a friend, is supposed to be coming over in a while."

"You need to get there as soon as possible. Call Gloria to come now; you can't stay here. Go upstairs and pack something light. I'll help get you out of here." He said, helping her to the staircase.

She carefully worked her way upstairs while he went to the room where Scott was killed to take pictures, hoping to find something the police might have missed. He got a broom and dustpan from the kitchen and went to the front, inside the French door, to clean up the broken shards of glass; he took it back to the kitchen garbage can only to notice a few seals on the kitchen counter. So, who broke the seal, and why did the police officer leave? He grabbed the torn seal endings after dumping the shards, trying to figure out what happened, but got nothing. He went through some drawers, found a hammer and some nails,

He heard Samantha's footsteps approaching the head of the staircase above him, and he walked back to the hall to meet her. He caught sight of the bracelet Blinky gave him lying on the floor and picked it up, feeling better about putting it on his wrist. "Thanks, Blinky," he whispered, picking up his hat.

When Samantha reached him, she was on her cell phone with Gloria, who said she would be right over. She still looked a little worse for wear. He asked her if there was anything to cover the pane where the glass was blown out. She even asked him how it happened while showing him some pieces of wood in the pantry under the steps. Jonathan grabbed a few thin, scrap ply pieces and quickly nailed them over the opening. As they went out on the brownstone steps, Jonathan correctly placed the seals on the doors and promised her he would stay until Gloria arrived. They sat on brownstone steps in the light of the early afternoon, feeling strange considering what had just occurred.

"My hand hurts, and I don't know why?" she said, rubbing her right hand, trying to soothe it with her other hand.

"I think you might have fallen on it when you fell," Jonathan stated while rubbing his chest, which was still smarting from the blow. He wondered if what brought her here had guided him here as well. For now, it was something he didn't want to spend too much time thinking over.

He decided he would ask her, "Why did you come back here?"

"Here?" she said, looking somewhat confused.

"Yes, back here where Scott died?"

She thought for a while and then padded a small suitcase, "Oh, I came back to get a few things; I remember going to the police station and asking if I could, and they brought me here with an officer. Wait, what happened to that nice officer, and how did the inside door glass break?"

"I think he left you here by yourself. Maybe he was called in or had to go somewhere. I couldn't tell you how the glass broke. Tell me, do you remember me coming to the door earlier and ringing your bell? You came and let me in."

"Err yes; you gave me your card, something about Raymond, Scott's brother, hiring you? It gets foggy from there." She put her hand on his and, in a sweet voice, said, "Guess I'm just lucky you came along."

He looked into her beautiful eyes, but before he could answer her, a car pulled up and was honking its horn; it was her friend Gloria. He helped her to the car with her bag. Gloria got out of the car to greet Samantha and introduced herself to Jonathan. "Hello, I'm Gloria Singleton. And you are?

"Err, Jonathan Hood, but you can call me Jonathan," he said, offering her his business card, which she delightfully accepted.

"Ooh, a private detective." I've never had one; I mean met one before." She said teasingly, blushing.

She was around Samantha's age, maybe a few years older, another looker causing Jonathan to give her his winning smile upon meeting her acquaintance. Samantha got in the car with Gloria, and Jonathan could see Gloria nudge her with one of those "Where-did-you-meet-him-from?" gestures. They drove away, leaving Jonathan to look back at the brownstone. It was still midday, and there weren't many people on the street, maybe one or two pedestrians walking their dogs down to Riverside Park. It was a good thing the front door pain didn't break; it would've caused a commotion and possibly a 911 call.

On the way back to his car, he concluded that whatever possessed Samantha must have influenced the officer to leave. The only thing he couldn't figure out for the moment was why did he assume she would be at the house? Was he drawn to her or attracted to the entity? He could've just merely asked Matthews where she was staying and went over to see her. How did he know she would be at the brownstone around this time and on this day? Too many damn coincidences,

When he reached his car, he looked at the pictures Jonathan took on his cell, not to study them but to make sure they were there; he would review them later. He sat in the car and collected himself; he had given Samantha the impression that he had control of the situation when in truth, he was unnerved by the whole state of affairs involving Scott's death, the specter in the mirror, and now the attack by something. As Jonathan sat there gazing out on West End Avenue, he could feel his hands begin to tremble uncontrollably. Was Scott involved in something else? Were Scott and Samantha engaged in ritual practices? Was Scott investigating a trail of circumstances different from Jonathan's that somehow affects people connected to him? Scott mentioned only being an accountant, but was there a side angle, something well-kept secret? He jotted some notes in his pad and decided to visit Mr. Sierra, the proprietor and antique dealer across town on the east side toward 1st Avenue.

Chapter 4

Sierra's Antique and Appraisal was the shop's name he walked into; Jonathan's chest was still a little sore from the blow at Samantha's place, and he would find himself rubbing it from time to time. The shop displayed beautiful and classic antique furniture. It held numerous shelves where delicate and expensive items sat on view

It was a corner shop with a corner front window allowing sunlight into the store. The bell rang after he entered as a short South America gentleman with salt and pepper hair and mustache, in his mid-fifties, came out from a desk in the back corner and maneuvered himself around a wooden and glass counter..

In a heavy Spanish accent, he asked, "What can I do for you today, sir?"

"Are you Mr. Sierra?"

"Si, err, yes. Francisco Sierra." He said, offering his hand.

"Did you know a Mr. Scott Simmons?" Jonathan asked as he handed him his business card.

Immediately Mr. Sierra lost his welcoming smile; his face took a painful, if not fearful, twist. "Scott? Err, yes. The police were here yesterday asking about him." He said, waving Jonathan off, not wanting anything to do with him; he didn't want to talk about it. "Please, Mr. Simmons was a very nice man. I really, no, no, I really can't talk about it." He removed himself from behind the counter and squirmed back toward his desk in the back corner of the store.

However, Jonathan wasn't about to let him get off that easy and followed him, continually prodding him with questions. Mr. Sierra finally stopped short in his tracks when Jonathan said, "Mr. Sierra, I'm worried about your welfare!"

Mr. Sierra quickly turned around, perspiration beginning to show on his forehead, "Why? What do you know?"

Jonathan realized that the shop area they were standing in held many full-length antique mirrors, and each one was draped with some heavy cloth.

"I know you've seen what I've seen," Jonathan said quietly as though a third party might be listening.

Mr. Sierra stepped back and wobbled back to his desk with Jonathan's assistance. He squeezed Jonathan's hand, "So, you've seen it too?" he asked, his voice shaking.

"Yes, I've seen it on several levels," Jonathan answered him, rubbing his chest.

Mr. Sierra sat in his desk chair while Jonathan sat in one of the two chairs designated for customers. Mr. Sierra appeared even smaller sitting behind his desk than he did standing. "There's no way the police would've believed me if I told them what was going on and what I saw; I'd be in Bellevue right now!"

Jonathan nodded, "Same here. Can I ask you a few questions? How did you know Scott?"

"He came into my store some weeks ago; he not only knew that I appraised items, but that I was once an archaeologist who also had degrees in anthropology and mythology.

"He wanted to set up a meeting for me to meet his boss, Mr. Robert Angler, president of his company. Mr. Angler, while vacationing in the Amazon rainforest last summer, came across a uniquely carved wooden idol, and he wanted it looked at by someone before taking it to anyone who might be willing to purchase it at a fair and marketable price."

He paused to pour himself some water, offering Jonathan a glass which Jonathan declined. He was more interested in hearing his story. After his drink, which helped to calm him down a bit, Mr. Sierra continued, "I told Mr. Simmons that I couldn't or wouldn't make any promises, for it's been quite a while since I practiced as an anthropologist. Mr. Simmons wasn't in the mood for doing a long, drawn-out search for Mr. Angler."

"So, when did you finally meet Mr. Angler?"

"I met him about a week ago. His limousine pulled up in front of my store, and his chauffeur helped him bring in the piece. It was just under three feet in length when he brought it wrapped. He asked his chauffeur to leave before he unveiled it. It was ancient and beautifully carved, early Incan and, it must have been part of an old, once standing, hard-wood tree, but the base had decayed."

He took out his handkerchief and wiped his forehead. "I asked him where the twin piece was. I would've been horrified if he had it, but he insisted that it was the only piece lying on the shoreline of the Amazon River. I presumed a flood or heavy rain must have carried it downstream where he. unfortunately, found it."

"Now. why would you have been horrified if he had both pieces, and why would he have been unfortunate in finding the one piece?" Jonathan asked.

"At the time when I first saw it, I was concerned, but I wasn't sure. I'm mean, even in my country of Ecuador, where I grew up, there were rumors and stories, no more, no less than other stories told to disobedient children across the world, right?" He froze for a second, staring into his nervous hands that shook as they moved across the desktop to reach the pitcher of water. Jonathan grabbed the glass picture; worried Mr. Sierra might knock it over, and poured some water for him. Mr. Sierra thanked him as he drew the glass toward him only to wind up staring into it as though there might have been something in the reflection looking back at him, and he couldn't break the gaze.

Jonathan had to break his trance, snapping his fingers and giving him a heightened bark, "Mr. Sierra, you were saying?"

Mr. Sierra looked at him with glassy eyes, "It was a guardián!"

"A what? Guardian?"

"Yes, yes, a guardian, a watcher," he began mumbling in non-stop Spanish, as though he couldn't believe the words coming from his mouth or the fact that it was the first time he spoke about it verbally to a stranger. His hands were waving all over the place as if he was trying to convince Jonathan and others in the shop, even though there was no one else in the store.

Jonathan grabbed his hands, trying to calm him down and reassure him with a soft tone in his voice, "It all right, Mr. Sierra, despacio por favor, despacio, cálmese, y en Inglés por favor," urging him to drink the glass of water.

Mr. Sierra regained control, apologized to Jonathan for his behavior, and tried to continue.

Jonathan helped him along, "You said, guardian?"

"Er, yes, like angelic beings, but in antiquity, people in ancient cultures would mark places on the earth, areas on the earth where they would decree temples should be built because wise and knowledgeable beings would advise them. Priests and shamans performed rituals around places where they recognized portals to another world as having to exist. In many societies, guardians would be erected where an evil place existed. They were used either as a warning to its inhabitance or as a guardian or guardians to seal the portal and keep unworldly beasts from entering into our realm. It was often taboo to even approach an area without the escort of a holy man, shaman, or priestess. Sadly, in some societies, such places would be used for sacrifices of young maidens or infants."

"And Mr. Angler's piece was such a guardian?"

"Yes, but I could tell by the carvings and the markings on it that it was one of two pieces, and if the other section is still there, then the portal is only half-opened."

Jonathan's dream flashed through his mind, and he remembered the one stone door being open with the beast chasing him as the opening pulled at him. He shook his head to rid himself of the image and went on listening to Mr. Sierra.

"I, like most of my colleagues, studied the stories, the legends, and the myths, but honestly never, did we believe such things were possible, not in the 21st century, but then I saw that horrid thing in my mirrors looking at me. Whatever that thing is, it has attached itself to the idol and the owner of the idol, to what end, I don't know, maybe it's his protector or something, God only knows." He finished with making the sign of the cross.

He had given Jonathan all that he could give him; he didn't want to tell him anything else. They both sat in their seats, and the silence was thick enough to stir it with a spoon. Suddenly the doorbell rang, causing both of them to jump out of their skins.

Two young men came into the store, one calling for Mr. Sierra, "Papa, you here, is everything okay?"

There was a sigh of relief in both Mr. Sierra and Jonathan, "Carlos, over here by the desk in the back." He yelled.

"It's my son, Carlos. He and his friend Daniel come by in the afternoon to check on me and the shop now that things are getting a little, how you say, 'hairy' around here." He smiled at Jonathan, with Jonathan commenting on how cool it was to have a son like that.

Carlos was his father's son, a young man in his mid-thirties who was only a few inches taller, more square, and weightier in body mass

"Who's he?" Carlos asked his father as he came closer, referring to Jonathan.

His father replied, "This is private detective Jonathan Hood. He's looking into the Scott Simmons' case."

From the look on Carlos' face, Jonathan could tell that he was getting heated, and his temper was about to flare. Carlos positioned himself closer to this father and tried to keep his voice down, but Jonathan overheard him anyway.

"Poppy, I told you not to discuss it with anyone, not anyone! Dejalo en paz! Leave it alone! Fuckin' stupido!" He rammed his finger into about an inch from Francisco's face.

Jonathan gave him a stern look, he was wrong about this kid, and this wasn't how his parents raised him; one didn't treat his father in such a tone of voice. He glanced over at Daniel, Carlos' friend, to gauge his response to the interaction. He was still near the counter, looking at them, just shrugging his shoulders and partially raising his hands in a show of non-involvement when he saw Jonathan looking at him as if to say he had nothing to do with their exchange.

Daniel, a young African American, was taller than Carlos. He looked like he could handle himself, definitely the quiet type who probably kept things close to the chest. His look at Carlos' interaction with his father also expressed to Jonathan that he might have felt Carlos was wrong in his treatment of his father.

Jonathan could feel the irritation getting to him, so he got up from his seat to leave. He had known too many asshole kids like him in his life, especially when on the force. He had had enough, he tapped Carlos on his shoulder, and Carlos angrily turned around to show he wasn't scared. Jonathan gave him a stern look and, with a firm voice, said, "If you want to talk to your father in that tone of voice when I'm not around, that's your business, but you will not speak to him that way; in front of me!"

Carlos raised his hand to strike Jonathan, but Jonathan grabbed his extended arm and twisted it behind him, slamming his face down on the desk.

Mr. Sierra jumped back, surprised by the loud sound it made. Daniel quickly stood up as if he would intervene; Jonathan looked back at him and shook his head with a don't-even-think-about-it expression. Daniel backed down.

"I apologize for this, Mr. Sierra, but I have a hard time tolerating disrespectful punks."

He turned and leaned over Carlos, twisting his arm further. Carlos was squirming in pain. Jonathan whispered in his ear, "You need to back off with your father. Do we have an understanding?"

Carlos grimaced while rapidly nodding his head.

Jonathan persisted with a little more pressure, "I said, do we have an understanding?"

Carlos cried out, "Yeah, yeah, shit yeah, damn you, you're breaking my fuckin' arm!"

Jonathan let him up and pushed him into one of the two chairs. He looked at Mr. Sierra, stuck out his hand in an offer of friendship while securing their acquaintance with his other palm in a gentlemanly fashion.

"It has been a pleasure talking with you. I hope we can do it again sometime." While shaking his hand, he looked over at Mr. Sierra's son, "Again, my apologies."

He tipped his hat to Carlos, "Carlos, 'til we meet again." Carlos automatically nodded his head, holding his right arm. Jonathan nodded to Daniel as he left the store.

In his car he felt a strange need to talk to Blinky. It was more of an urge but somehow felt right.

The ride uptown would consist of a replay of Mr. Sierra's story concerning portals, guardians, and sacrifices. After parking his car a few blocks away, he walked to Blinky's spot. His thoughts poured over the incident involving Carlos Sierra's behavior toward his father to act in that manner. Was he being overly protective and didn't want his father depicted as crazy? Still, the energy behind it didn't feel right; it wasn't necessary for a son who claimed he cared for his father and yet treated him that way. It was like he was possessed, and Lord knows Jonathan had enough of that today.

A block away and looking down the avenue, he could see there stood a large crowd, an ambulance and police cars with lights flashing, some car accident had occurred. A vehicle had swerved off the avenue and ran up on the corner right where Blinky sat. It was a moment of disbelief, and he started running up to the scene. When he got there, Blinky was missing from his post. He felt a wave of unsettling anxiety sweep over him when he saw the car's fender rammed into the concrete corner of the bar with Blinky's seat crushed underneath. Emergency Rescue was tending to someone. He took a quick look; it was an older adult. A new type of stress was beginning to weigh on him; it was still late in the afternoon and sunny. What was the hell going on? Too many damn coincidences!

Chapter 5

Jonathan talked with some of the foot soldiers writing up the accident report. The elderly gentleman was the only injured party. He went into the bar and asked Larry, the bartender, if he had seen Blinky. He pointed toward the corner, and Jonathan turned around.

Blinky was sitting at a table in the corner sipping on a glass of seltzer water, looking a little pissed behind the dark shades he wore, but a lot healthier than had he'd been at his post. Jonathan went to him and padded Blinky's shoulder, shaking it warmly; he wasn't much of a hugging type of person For him, it was about the most emotion he was going to show as their relationship growing up might've been close, but never that close.

"Blinky, thank God you're okay! I was worried like hell coming up the block and seeing the commotion outside. Let me buy you something to drink."

"Sure, I'll have a White Russian."

"What's with you and the Russians?" Jonathan joked.

Blinky smiled at the pun.

Jonathan was just relieved to know that Blinky was okay, and as he was feeling awkward about it and the level of his concern, he had to make sure he didn't chatter too much. As he went to get the drinks, he could hear him telling himself, "Calm down."

Jonathan brought the drinks and sat back down with Blinky, "So where were you when the car slammed into your spot?"

"I was resting quietly, as usual, when nature called, and it was a good thing I heard her. I just got up and came in here when 'BAM!'" He took a sip of his drink and smiled.

"Wow, somebody's watching over you."

"Don't I know it," Blinky responded, raising his glass and peering upward and across the room.

After they mused over another one or two libations flavored with memories of some of the near misses in their lives and small talk that helped fill the lulls in their conversation, Jonathan asked him if they could go out and talk more seriously about today's events. When they left out of the bar, the earlier crowd of onlookers had watered down out to only a few folks, a few officers, and a tow truck that was hoisting away the damaged vehicle.

They went to the park around the corner. The sun was making its move toward the western horizon. Jonathan assisted Blinky to a bench where Jonathan spent a little while trying to figure out where, to begin with, his story.

He pulled his coat sleeve back to show Blinky that he was now wearing the bracelet he had given him. "Thanks, this was probably a lifesaver for me today, literally." From there, he would recount what happened at the brownstone with Samantha Simmons. As he told his tale, he could see Blinky's eyebrows dance behind his dark shades. He could see that Blinky would, now and then, look around their area as if to make sure they were alone, even though there were people visible to both of them.

After the story involving Samantha, Jonathan went into what he had heard and learned from Mr. Sierra concerning his connection with the late Scott Simmons. He talked about Scott's role in finding an appraiser and anthropologist for the totem and how Mr. Angler had discovered it in the Amazon forest. He left out the behavior of Mr. Sierra's son, Carlos, but he segued the story into the dream he had dreamt the night before.

By the time Jonathan was nearing the end of his tale, the sky behind them had begun to darken. Blinky grabbed his arm and stopped him mid-sentence.

"Let's pick this up in my apartment. Do you mind coming over?" Blinky asked.

Jonathan nodded but then realized that he never knew where he lived after all the years of growing up with Blinky. He helped Blinky to his feet, and suddenly somewhat embarrassed, he exclaimed, "Blinky, err, where do you live?"

Blinky never laughed so hard all day; he almost fell back on the bench, losing his balance. Jonathan had to keep him on his feet.

"Oh, you're good, perfect, Detective Hood!" he said sarcastically with emphasis, adding a sharp salute in his direction. "Dunbar Projects."

"Oh, right over there?" Even Jonathan burst out with laughter, thinking about how long he had known Blinky. "My bad!"

They both walked down the block in heated laughter that cooled down when they reached the avenue.

Blinky motioned for them to stop as he took a moment to reach in his bag and pull out his cell phone; he had his home phone on speed dial and wanted to let his mate know he was bringing a friend named Jonathan to the house. He finished his call with an "Okay? Yeah, yeah, okay. We'll be there shortly."

"Blinky, honestly, I didn't know you were married? When did this happen?" Jonathan asked.

"Oh, we're not married in the legal sense of the word. We met each other about eight years ago at a function where we found we had some things in common, the way most heart-drawn folks do."

"Do I know her? How come you never mentioned her?"

A smile beamed on Blinky's face because Jonathan had no clue where he lived, and now he was questioning him about a lady friend. "I never mentioned her before because you never ask."

Jonathan's face went blank, Blinky was full of surprises, but then he thought to himself. *It's not Blinky's fault, realizing he needed to get more involved with some of the folks in the neighborhood, people he claimed to know when in reality he didn't know shit about them. He had a bad habit of holding himself aloft from others. He found himself apologizing to Cindy, who often stated that as a detective, he kept too many secrets which kept him at a distance from friends and the common folk.*

"You're right there; I won't argue about that. By any chance, do I know her? What does she do? What's her name?" He picked up the questioning as they entered a Dunbar Project archway on the avenue.

"Joey to me, short for Joanna. I don't know if you know her, though you might have seen her in the neighborhood. She's a healer, works as a nurse over at Harlem Hospital in the Emergency Room."

They worked their way through the quiet interior of the project until they came to Blinky's building. They walked to the third floor. Jonathan remembered scampering through these projects as a young child with his buddies back in the day. He had to admit, though, he never really knew anyone who claimed to live here. It always seemed like a place secluded from the surrounding community.

When the door opened, they were greeted by a woman with dreads in her mid-thirties, obviously of Jamaican heritage with a cute, clean face, wearing a white dress, white beads with a few other strands of colored beads, and a white cloth tied around her head.

When Jonathan saw her, he realized he knew her as Nurse Paterson in Harlem Hospital's emergency room, where he used to go as a detective to question victims. She seemed to bubble over with gladness to see a friend of Blinky.

Her voice was joyful and appealing, "Hello, hello, oh my God, we know each other from the E.R. Detective Hood, how are you, my, my, what a small world." She giggled and pointed to his shoes.

"Small world indeed," he answered, delighted she was someone he knew, so he wouldn't have to succumb to the awkward process of introductions. He noticed Blinky removing his shoes at the door before entering and placing them on a shoe rack outside the door in the hallway. He followed suit and started taking his footwear off. He knelt, thinking he would greet her with a kiss on the chick when he finished. Meanwhile, while he was down, taking off his last shoe, she took a steep swig of rum from a bottle she held in her hand behind the door and held the swig in her mouth waiting.

When he rose up and leaned in to place that kiss, she let loose with an explosive spray of rum from her mouth onto his face, immediately followed with a quick prayer-blessing asking for protection for this child of God, amen!

"What the...?" he yelled, stumbling back in total surprise.

She apologized, "Sorry, but there was a good amount of negative residue still on you from whatever happened today, and I just couldn't let you bring it into our home."

Blinky handed him a white cloth to wipe his face. The spray definitely caught him off guard, but he couldn't help but quietly snicker because he had heard of such things, but this was a first for him. He tasted the rum around his lips, "Hmm, could you put some of this in a glass?" which brought them all to ease.

She presented him with a small cup of rum as he entered the doorway. He wiped his mouth area and gave her that kiss he had intended. "Nice meeting you. Joey?" he pointed at her, making sure he was right.

"Joey, it is," she responded with a slight curtsy, "Are you hungry? I was fixing something for Robert when he called."

"If it's not too much trouble, I'd be extremely grateful." He knew his manners when needed.

Blinky escorted him to his living room where they sat on a cornered couch, while Joey went back into the kitchen, Jonathan secured a quick scan of the apartment, very well kept, with a decent size alter in the western corner of the room to catch the rays of the rising sun. There were bits and pieces of African, Jamaican, and Afro-Brazilian artifacts all around him. It was a side of Blinky or Robert he had never known.

Jonathan began feeling awkward about even referring to Robert as Blinky, especially at his house in front of his mate. He decided to ask him, "Is calling you 'Blinky' okay with you, coming from me? And sadly, I must say, I've always known you as Blinky. What is your full name?"

"Robert Conyers and sure, Joey doesn't mind. She has her nicknames from her childhood that she keeps with a certain number of her friends. Err, excuse me, I need to change, be right back." He stepped out of the room.

Jonathan noticed a decent size collection of books on the far wall; a good number of them looked like they were printed in braille for Blinky. This quiet kid, who he and other friends of his made fun of, was someone other than anyone one of them had ever thought he'd be. Jonathan was impressed by the surroundings and the energy he could feel from this apartment. Whatever was troubling him earlier seemed to vanish in this space.

Blinky came back into the room wearing white clothes and sandals; he had a pair of flip-flops for Jonathan to put on his feet. Blinky had a book he wanted to show Jonathan in his hand. "This book, which Joey reads to me called, 'Conversations with Mama Maneya,' holds a slightly different approach to the concept of what Mr. Sierra was telling you. When referring to the creatures from 'dark portals as demons,' it may not have been a demon, at least as most people would call it." Blinky sounded like a well-educated professor at some university of higher learning. His whole manner changed, the rapid blinking continued behind his shades, but he was no longer the same person the neighborhood knew on that street corner, begging for change.

"What do you mean, because it felt like some demon to me?"

Blinky sat there and looked at him for a second, "Honestly, Johnny, if you don't mind me saying so, I didn't know you were a professional because you sound like someone familiar with seeing demons."

"Well, I wouldn't go that far," he answered. Then he saw Blinky smiling at him and said, "Never mind, I get your point."

"Even so, it may be a beast of some kind, a beast from another realm or dimension; the way a beast might appear in our dimension, like a tiger, a lion, or a crocodile."

"You mean like from a jungle in another place? Still, you should realize that it spoke to me."

"Yeah, like while there are intelligent life forms in our realm, there are intelligent life forms in other realms. When an enlightened being from another realm is a 'crossover,' that portal may be deemed sacred, as Mr. Sierra was explaining to you, allowing for the building of temples and such. However, when a beast from another realm becomes a 'crossover,' its doorway or portal may align itself to an area of jungle in that other world and as in all forests throughout the universe. The hunt is always on, and whatever skills it uses to hunt, defend or kill may be to its advantage in our realm, even having access to mimicking the language or speech of the person it inhabits. Of course, it's all speculation on my part."

"Its behavior, while natural to the realm it comes from, is unnatural for us and is labeled as negative or demonic to us. Is this what you're saying?" Jonathan said, making an effort to understand Blinky's explanation.

"There are times when humans and beasts from our realm crossover into theirs. There may be advantages or disadvantages to either realm, an example being the fragrance attached to the bracelet I gave you. It may very well be potent enough on their level to hurt or harm them physically or psychically while smelling sweet and alluring to us."

"Hmm, so why is this 'beast' attached to the idol and its owner?

"Now that's something I couldn't tell you, maybe it was the first of a group to come out of the portal and has somehow become attached to it, thinking by staying close to it and protecting the one who has it, it can find its way back. I couldn't say for sure. Still, we must keep in mind that if enlightened beings can come through, so can the unenlightened, bent on doing whatever. As long as that portal remains open to wherever it is currently connected, other beasts may come through, some by accident, maybe even some with intent."

"Can those unenlightened be any eviler than some of the humans from our realm?"

"Exactly my point Jonathan, the pendulum swings both ways. One could argue that some humans are the evilest creatures in this realm, if not on this planet, particularly since cruelty and injustice is a natural byproduct of our species."

Jonathan sat back on the couch; he had heard enough as he handed the book back to Blinky. He started working on a plan in his head to find somehow a way to locate that idol and get it back to the proper authorities if such a thing was possible.

Joey entered the room with three folding trays and handed them Jonathan, who set up one for each of them. She called to him and asked if he could come to get the drinks and eating utensils. She followed him back into the living room with a steaming hot plate of food and came back with two more, serving herself last.

"I hope you don't mind, but we don't eat meat." She said as she took a seat.

"No, it's okay. Thank you, it smells delicious," and it was. Jonathan, Blinky, and Joey spent the next hour talking about their origins, the neighborhood, along with the small talk necessary for weaving together a new bond of friendship and trust. Their apartment was like a small museum of art pieces, photographs, and Joey was kind enough to point out specific artworks and the meaning and history behind them.

Joey knew he wanted to ask her about the altar, considering how now and then his eyes would steer their way to that corner of the room. So, she pointed to it and said, "Questions?"

He asked, "Santeria, Vodun?"

"There be roots there, but there be roots from other places for the tree be mighty." She added an extra Jamaican twang to her voice.

Blinky smiled; he enjoyed Joey's energy as he guessed at Jonathan's innate response, considering Jonathan's upbringing in the west under Christian doctrine. Joey chuckled at Blinky as she collected the dishes to take into the kitchen to wash.

When she left the room, Jonathan turned to Blinky and sat down close to him said quietly, "Blinky, seeing you like this is different from the way you appear on the corner asking for change. Why do you do that?"

"I'm doing my part in a small way; from there, I can see, hear, feel, and hopefully touch and heal some of the suffering souls and spirits around us. You'd be surprised to know that with the right intention or a loving heart, just by shaking a hand or offering a kind word, how much healing one can do. Do you think I care if folks see me in a bad light? Even if by seeing my state, they can feel more blessed, then that small degree of good adds to the fabric of our being."

"And by spirits, you mean ghosts?"

"Spirits occupying vessels and those without, does it matter? There's so much more beyond the veil of our understanding. I'm not about to get on a soapbox and preach my slant on things, for who knows, maybe my mother was right, and it's all in my imagination. So, let's keep it simple and don't try to put more food on the plate than folks can eat."

"Do any other folks around here know what you do?"

"Only those Joey and I council from time to time, but they know enough to keep things to themselves when considering their relationship with us. After all, we only are of service to those who understand our approach enough to allow us into their lives."

Jonathan stood up, rubbing his head in wonderment. "Well, I must say I'm at a loss for words. Blinky, it makes me feel bad about all those pranks me and the other guys played on you. You're somewhat of a special individual. You must've thought we were hooligans to the max."

"You were kids, no more, no less than I was. It was strange, but somehow I was often amused by the fact that you guys picked me to be your straight man."

"You mean the brunt of our jokes."

Blinky shooed him away, "Ah, water under the bridge."

"Chance and time certainly had their hands in the mix when it came to putting us two together." Jonathan took one last look around the apartment; he always felt uncomfortable expressing his goodbyes when he thought he wanted to stay longer at a place. "Well, this has certainly been an eye-opener, but I got to get going."

Joey brought out his hat and coat. "Jonathan, it was a pleasure having you over; please feel free to drop by any time."

"I would love to, and thanks for a marvelous meal, Joey," he said, giving her a peck on her cheek.

He turned to Blinky, "It's been great, see you when I see you. Okay?"

"Okay."

Joey saw him to the door, and as he was leaving and handed him a small package that he was able to fit in his coat pocket, she then said, "The day isn't over yet, so be careful out there," she said, giving him a look that reminded of a look his mother would give.

"Will do." He waved, wondering – *now what could she mean by that?* – He continued down the stairs.

Joey went back inside to Robert, "A good man, but I can tell he's got a quiet temper that's rumbling just below the surface. Keep your eye out for him; he's gonna need you sooner than later."

Blinky nodded and smiled to himself; the idea amused him, so now the blind guy has to keep an eye out on a sighted person.

Chapter 6

It was evening, and Jonathan came out of an entrance on 150th Street, walked down to Macombs Place, turned up the avenue as he wanted to walk off some of the day's events. Just ahead of him was an attractive young woman in a short, red, fake-leather jacket that hugged her waist beautifully accentuated her hips that wove into two shapely legs.

Suddenly from behind him, he heard a rustle of footsteps; he could feel a rush of adrenalin gush up his spine. From the corner of his eye, he gathered three dark figures were coming up from behind, with one of them closing in on him. He ducked just as a crowbar went flying over his head.

He threw his foot back hard against the man's knee only to hear a loud crack mixed with a painful groan as the man went down. Jonathan rolled over and drew his revolver. A second man had his gun drawn, Jonathan instantly shot twice, hitting him square in the chest and throwing him back onto the hood of a parked car only to slide off and fall limp between two vehicles.

The woman turned around paralyzed and just started screaming hysterically. The third man just waylaid her with a hard right, "Shut up, bitch!" She went down as he rushed over to Jonathan with a large hunting knife, kicking the gun out of Jonathan's hand before Jonathan could get a fix on him. He dove on top of Jonathan, intentionally using his weight to help plunge the blade into the region of his face or neck.

It took all the strength Jonathan could muster, but he caught him as he fell, the blade only an inch or so away from his face. They struggled for what seemed forever. The thug relaxed enough to pull back and again tried to plunge the blade into Jonathan. In that instant, Jonathan grabbed a pencil from his inside pocket and swiftly jabbed it into the guy's left eye, breaking it off on the thug's socket.

The man found an agonizing voice he never thought would come from him as it exploded into the darkness around them. Meanwhile, the first thug did his best to get back on his feet, working his way toward Jonathan swinging his crowbar. Jonathan scrambles to his feet, picks up the dropped hunting knife, and hurls it hard, hitting the thug just above his groin; he goes down.

Jonathan hurries over to where his gun is and picks it up, checking the scene around him. The last assailant is seen moaning and squirming on the sidewalk. Jonathan goes over to the young woman and checks on her, cradling her bruised head as sirens are racing from every direction and windows from nearby apartments are opening with folks peering out onto the scene. A car runs off into the darkness toward the Bronx.

He stays kneeling with the woman, keeping his gun on the third attacker while placing her head in his lap. Two police cars pull up with an ambulance. As the officers step onto the curb, Jonathan puts his gun down, points to the assailant, and places his hands behind his head.

One of the officers recognizes him, "Hood, what the hell? Just can't keep your ass out of trouble, eh?"

Jonathan shrugged his shoulders, "Just put the call in for the rest of this mess." He wasn't in the mood.

After a while, two more unmarked cars pulled up. Matthews and Samuels stepped out of one of them and came over to take a quick look at the bodies, with Matthews scratching his head at the bloodshed.

"Hey, this guy is Patch Morgan, one of Syd Barnes goons!" yelled Samuels to Matthews.

"Yeah, this guy is too, but I don't recognize him yet." He said, raising his flashlight off the perpetrator's face.

"Detective Matthews? We got a live one over here," said one of the officers pointing at the perp with the broken pencil in his eye.

"Jacob 'Deep Blade' Williams, well I'll be damned, finally got your ass. Put his ass on a stretcher." Matthews said, calling the EMS operators. He shook his head while working his way over to Jonathan and whispering in his ear, "Damn good work!"

The doors of the second unmarked car flew open, and out came Captain Mark Henderson with a lieutenant. He immediately began pointing at Jonathan, "Why isn't that man in cuffs? God damn it, I said, why isn't that man in cuffs?"

Matthews turned to him, "Err, sir? These guys are all Syd Barnes' boys; looks pretty much like they were out to do a hurting on Mr. Hood."

"I don't give a fuck what it looks like to you! There's a shooting, and until it's resolved, I want that bastard in cuffs and his ass taken downtown." He walked over to Jonathan and glared in his face like a man who wanted to hurt him. He was shorter than Jonathan, with a darker complexion. Henderson had a stuffy, blunt, and heavy-set stature that made him look tight in his clothes. He seemed to purposely wear them one size too small as if to make him look like he was busting out, just proud of himself, and wanted everyone else around him to know his importance because he looked different from anyone else. The look was pathetic as far as Jonathan was concerned.

Jonathan was unmoved; he just stared at Henderson's broken nose while the officer cuffed him. Jonathan realized Henderson never got it fixed since he broke several years ago. "Glad to see you too, Capt.," Jonathan said, smiling at him.

"Yeah, and I like your new look. Get Mr. Hood out of here!" Henderson ordered.

As they led Jonathan away, he turned and said, "No matter, this ain't gonna fix your nose."

Captain Henderson charged at him, cursing but was held back by Matthews and his assistant, who needed to calm him down and direct him toward the camera lights and press that were beginning to gather.

Just as the officers placed Jonathan in the police car, he saw Joey at the edge of the gathering crowd. Looking back at him, she must've ventured out after hearing all the sirens blaring throughout the neighborhood, and then she turned her gaze to Henderson and offered him a look of disdain as though she knew him.

As the police car slowly turned around to head downtown amidst the flashing lights, he saw Henderson catch sight of Joey in the crowd before reaching the press; he could see her waving him off in disgust and walking back to the projects. Henderson just stood there for a second with a "what-did-I-do-wrong-now?" expression.

Jonathan immediately picked up a history between them. She caught Jonathan's eyes as he rode away and gave a gentle bow of her head, for she was right about one thing, the day for him wasn't over.

He realized just how wrong he was about Barnes on the ride down. One day out and he was about keeping promises. He thought it would take him longer to act against him, considering he just got out of prison. Then again, maybe he needed to prove he was a man of his word to his peers, so Barnes just decided to order the hit on Jonathan to show he still had some clout. Jonathan was hard-pressed to believe Barnes' legal counsel would've agreed with such a move so early after his release, but then again, Syd was always a hothead.

When he reached the station, Matthews and Samuels just pulled up next to the patrol car; they told the arresting officer, "We'll take it from here, and we'll process him." He started to object, but they gave him a look that told him not to get in their way.

They grabbed Jonathan under the arms, one on each side, marching him into the precinct, "Hey man, what's the real deal between you and Capt.?" Samuels asked.

"It's a long, long drawn out story, and unless you guys are willing to sit in a cell with me for a few hours, it ain't worth talkin' about it now, maybe someday over coffee, or maybe we can go to the park and have a picnic."

As they brought him through the yard, there were a lot of cheers, greetings, and waves from fellow officers, "Hey, Hood, how you doin'?" "Good to see ya, buddy?" "What's been going on?" "Nice job on Barnes' goons, why to go!"

It was reminiscent of an old, admired sports star walking into his home arena. Hood was popular and well-liked when he was on the force; even though he was one to stay much to himself, he had their respect. Everyone there had their take, their own story on what the relationship between Hood and Henderson was all about. Yet, they held their opinions close to the chest. Since the captain was still uptown enjoying the limelight of the press, they could treat Jonathan as a human being, something they knew they couldn't do if the Capt. Henderson was on the grounds.

After processing and taking Jonathan's statement about what took place at the scene, they put him in a cell by himself. He sat there working out a possible relationship between Joey (Joanna) and Mark Henderson. As far as he was concerned, she appeared to know him and he, her. Still, Henderson was an asshole, and he wasn't about to waste time sitting in some damn cell trying to think over that asshole's life.

They grew up in Harlem together and knew each other from junior high school. Mark had always been an insecure seeker of fame and glory, only one who never truly earned it, spending his time climbing on the backs of everyone around him. He'll never change, Jonathan thought.

He looked around him, looking at the names over the badges familiar to him and the ones new to the "house" since he left. There was a smell to the place, especially in the area he was in, that brought back memories, nothing fond, nothing warm, just memories – enough to remind him just how glad he was to have gotten the hell out of this place.

After about an hour, Matthews came by with a cup of coffee and offered it to Jonathan; he took a sip, spitting some of it out, "Damn! What the —? Some things never change; I guess shit will always taste like shit!" He handed the cup back to Matthews, who just drank the rest without flinching, nonchalantly shrugging his shoulders.

He just leaned in closer to the bars and whispered, "Did you find anything about the Simmons case? Anything you're willing to share because as any news would have it, we're a little stuck down here."

Jonathan realized he couldn't tell Matthews about the 'demon,' so he asked him about Mr. Sierra first, "Did Francisco Sierra tell you anything?"

"Mr. Sierra? We got nothing out of Mr. Tight Lips. Did you notice all the mirrors in his place covered with drapes and shit? What's up with that? What did he tell you?"

"Eh, not much. When I started talking to him, his son came in took over the interview, basically telling his father to keep his damn mouth shut. It was weird."

Jonathan thought about telling Matthews about Samantha being at the crime scene, but he dismissed the urge. He still couldn't get a grip on what it was that drew him to her in the first place; he realized it was also something that he had kept from Blinky.

As they were talking, the conversation was slam-blasted with, "What the hell is he doing in that cell by himself? He's nobody special, just a-freakin' gumshoe, down on his luck like any other two-bit bum out there on the street. Put his ass with the stupid pieces of shit!" It was Henderson, back in the house.

Matthews had the jailor open the door and took Jonathan out when Samuels, who seemingly came out of nowhere, urgently worked his way up to Capt. Henderson and whispered something in his ear.

Henderson turned to Matthews, "Wait! Bring his ass into my office! Pronto! And you too Matthews, both you and Samuels come into my office."

The eyes of everyone in the immediate area followed them as they walked into Capt. Henderson's office, whereafter he slammed the door loud and hard.

The captain threw himself in his chair while pointing for Jonathan to sit in the wooden chair across from him. "Alright, Mr. Hood, exactly where were you around 5:30 p.m. this evening?"

Matthews and Samuels positioned themselves on either side of Jonathan just in case he had planned on going somewhere, not that he was, but it was more a show of strength for the captain.

Jonathan looked at Henderson and rubbed his chin as if going over the day's events. "I was uptown."

"That's not good enough."

"Good enough for what?"

"Good enough for this." He opened a file recently placed on his desk. There were glossies of a butchered body sprawl across the deck of what appeared to be a cargo vessel. As with Scott Simmons' death, there were numerous unrecognizable symbols drawn in blood all around the corpse.

Captain Henderson slammed his fingers on the photos, "How well did you know Scott Simmons and those connected to him? I don't think this is a coincidence."

Jonathan looked more closely at the photos, but he had no words for Henderson. "Honestly, I don't know who he is, but if he was still holding that machete after that carnage, my first guess is that he must've put up one hell of a fight."

Captain Henderson slapped the top of his desk, "Personally, I don't give a shit what you think! It's Capt. Joseph Walker, of a cargo shipping company that worked at the same company that Scott Simmons worked, his name, like yours was on one the business cards found on at the Simmons crime scene."

"I'm sorry, sir, but I didn't know about any other business cards at the crime scene (covering up his meeting with Matthews earlier). I only found out about Scott Simmons from Detectives Matthews and Samuels the other day when they came to see me."

Samuels nodded his head.

"Yeah, and they should've brought your ass in like I told them to, but they seem to have found better things to do with their time." Henderson added, grimacing at both of them and then continuing with Jonathan, "Now you still haven't answered my question. Where were you earlier this evening, around five?"

"I did tell you, I was uptown."

"You didn't tell me about it to my satisfaction. Can you corroborate it?"

"You mean do I have an alibi?" he answered with an eyebrow raised and smiling at Mark, something he used to do when they were in junior high school together.

"You're a smart ass, Johnny; you know that? Yeah, I mean alibi." Henderson knew Jonathan hated being called that name by anyone but a few choice souls.

Jonathan looked at him hard but wasn't about to let it phase him. "I was uptown with some friends."

"Names, damn it, names! I'm tired of dealing with your horse-shit attitude. I want names!"

"Alright, Robert 'Blinky' Conyers, and" he paused long enough for Henderson's body to shift in "anticipation mode" to get the effect he wanted. 'Joanna 'Joey' Paterson."

It had the effect Jonathan had expected, catching Henderson totally off guard. He stopped abruptly and started a choking fit that slowly grew louder the longer it went.

"Spit go down the wrong pipe, Capt.?" Jonathan queried.

Henderson did his best to normalize his condition, finally accepting a cup of water from Samuels, who had retrieved it from his office cooler.

In a gritty voice, purposely kept low so the others might not hear him, he leaned across his desk toward Jonathan, "How do you know Ms. Paterson?"

Jonathan, not caring who else in the room might've heard him, repeated the question at an audible volume, "What? How do I know Miss Paterson?" emphasizing each word.

"Well, if I could use your phone, I could call Robert, and he could let her confirm that I was with them earlier around that time." He didn't know Blinky's number offhand; he just dealt out a bluff to gauge Captain Henderson's response.

"Err, that won't be necessary. I don't need to talk to Ms. Paterson."

Jonathan thought to himself, You mean, you don't want to talk to her.

There was a knock on the Captain's door; Samuels opened it to accept an incident report. He takes a quick glance at it.

Samuels handed it to Captain Henderson, who took a moment to review it. He began shaking his head, obviously disappointed at the information in front of him. He slowly looked up at Jonathan, "Hmm, Mr. Hook, it appears that you were justified in discharging your weapon at the incident on Macombs Place. As of this moment, you're released. You're free to go, see to retrieving your property; you know the drill."

Jonathan got up in a businesslike manner; he didn't want to stir the waters any longer. He was definitely sure there was something between Joey and Henderson at some point in the past. He gave a quick nod to the captain and the others in the room and left them to go to the Property Clerk's window and retrieve his belongings.

When Jonathan left, Henderson called the Property Clerk's and Desk Sargent's extension and told them to do the long-extended version on Jonathan's release papers.

"So, what do you think, Matthews?" Henderson asked.

"We need to keep him on a tight leash, who knows; maybe he can be of some use to us." Of course, Matthews was saying what he thought the captain wanted to hear; he didn't think to take him seriously.

"Excellent idea. Starting tomorrow, you and Samuels stay on him, as close as possible to see what he's up to."

"Sir, we're still working the Simmons' case. You want us to get off it?"

Captain Henderson calmed himself; he didn't want Matthews to think that his grievance with Hood was becoming something personal and that he might be losing his objectivity.

"You're right, of course. I'll get Louis and Rodriguez to keep an eye on him. When did they come on the force?"

"About six months before Hood left for Rodriguez and Louis came in after Hood left."

"Good, then he may not recognize them. Meanwhile, have a patrol sent over to Ms. Judith Andrew and Mr. Francisco Sierra's for protection, the artist and antique dealer whose name was on the business cards found on Simmons' body. I heard the chiropractor was out of town. Am I right.?"

They nodded.

"Yes, on it, sir. Err, sir?" Samuels added.

"You got something to say, Samuels? Henderson said to Samuels.

"What about Mr. Hood?"

"What about him?"

"His name was also on one of the business cards found at the crime scene."

"And?"

"Well, shouldn't he receive some protection as well?"

"He can take care of himself, besides I got Louis and Rodriguez tailing him. So, any more questions?"

"Err, no."

"Alright, then."

The Property Officer at the claims window was taking his sweet time with Jonathan, having him sign for each piece in triplicate.

Jonathan caught on right away, "Oh, so this is how it's gonna be, Ed, eh?" folding his arms in an unsatisfied display.

The officer shrugged his shoulders and then decided to speed up the process despite the captain's orders, at least not as slow as he was previously going.

By the time Jonathan left the precinct station, it was 1:34 in the morning. He would have to take the iron horse back uptown, leaving him to wonder what the deal or arrangement was with this precinct and the precinct at 147th street. That precinct was closest to the shooting scene. Maybe Henderson had worked out something since Simmons's case was in his district. Knowing Henderson, the Capt must have some foot soldiers keeping an eye on him, considering how fast Henderson arrived at the shooting scene. He turned to take one last look while nearing the exit, his eyes falling on Samuels on his cell phone. Samuels' dumpy face looked upset with whoever was on the line, he looked up in time to see Jonathan wave him goodnight, but upon seeing Jonathan, he turned around as if to avoid him. Jonathan didn't know what to make of it. He just shrugged his shoulders and went about his business, needing to get home.

Once he felt he was outside the shadow of the station, the presence of the night pressed down on him. His thought process dictated the pace in which he strode, measuring out the distance between him and the train station. He did a quick reality check of the area around him, the space between people, and their surrounding space. The silence with droplets of traffic and city noise held a flavor of its own, reminding of Joey's words about the day not yet being over.

His thoughts turned to the photos of Capt. Joseph Walker of the freight ship. *The creature was keeping busy, and the vessel captain had a machete. If the beast needed to possess someone to kill the captain, then it is quite possible that poor soul whose body it used was cut and severely wounded somewhere in the neighborhood of the docks or at a hospital close by with no memory of what happened. Who did it possess to kill Simmons?*

This creature may be more intelligent than Blinky might have realized, at least on a level of intelligence measured on its realm compared to ours. Why is it trying to cover its tracks, or is someone else knowingly or unknowingly manipulating it for some evil purpose?

He even entertained the thought that maybe the senses of that particular type of creature had a totally different sensory system. *It could be possible that it could sense the connection of the people involved, the way a spider can perceive things connected to its web, or maybe Mr. Angler was trying to cover his tracks for illegally bringing the idol through customs and is now seeking to erase everyone attached. After all, the evil of humans is probably on par with the evil anywhere else in the universe. If we all could commit undetected crimes against each other, we probably would. Maybe it was doing what came naturally to it.*

He entered the subway and found himself cautiously stepping over and around a few homeless people. "This is a whole 'nother level of violence." He thought to himself, looking back at them when he reached the turnstile.

By the time he reached the platform level, the number of scattered vagrants were everywhere, one here, one way over there, and so on. The New York electrical subway smell of live wires mixed with stale body odor. Then there was that subway hum way down in the belly of the tunnel, the sound of something approaching. He looked down the tunnel and saw headlights drawing near.

When the train pulled into the station, he took the seat in the middle car. It had been quite a while since he traveled by train. The life of a transit rider gradually dissipates until it finally vanishes, fading into fable once one becomes a car owner.

"Due to police work on 125 Street station, next stop on this train is 145 Street," came an announcement on the platform. *Okay, by me,* Jonathan thought.

When he took a seat, he immediately did a headcount of the number of people in the car. There were four other riders, including the police officer at the other end of the subway car. Jonathan started doing what most typical New Yorkers do when riding the train. He glances at the advertisements along the top edge of the ceiling, only to settle down on the full poster across from him, and there it was, looking at him, a shapeless form glaring at him off the plexiglass cover. He made a move for his gun only to stop short, realizing it would have little to no effect on it.

It shifted to his right and went from out of his view; suddenly, a middle-aged black man of about 225 lbs got up and charged him, screaming. Jonathan swiftly moved to his side as the man's head rammed into the metal armrest. He slumped to the floor out cold.

Everyone else in the car jumped, but before he had time to check on the individual, an elderly brown-skin woman came at him with a sharp pair of scissors that she pulled out of her purse, mumbling incoherently at him. Jonathan got up, grabbed the pole, swung out of her way, causing her to trip and fall with the scissors flying down the car. She lay near the man who had fallen, unconscious!

Jonathan realized this creature was jumping from person to person, using them as weapons at its disposal.

Next, a heavy-set, built-like-a-truck white teen came at him. He could certainly handle himself; at least, that was what Jonathan surmised. As he got up, somewhat taller than Jonathan, and ran at him, Jonathan made quick work of landing as many blows as possible, which had little to no effect. The stranger had his fists up, and Jonathan knew he was about to feel some severe pain. Jonathan just grabbed the kid and flew past him, causing him to hit his skull on the hard-plastic seat, cracking it. He was out, leaving Jonathan exhauste0d and trying to catch his breath.

The police officer was on top of Jonathan with his gun drawn. Yelling at him to get up and place his hands behind his head, he complied. Jonathan faced him and pleaded, "Officer, it wasn't my fault, for some reason, they all came at me!"

Suddenly, something about the officer's character changed, reminding him of Samantha's I-got-you-now look. He saw his mouth twist as he slowly cocked his gun.

Jonathan swiftly grabbed his arm, turned him around, and put him in a chokehold. As they struggled, the bracelet progressed up Jonathan's wrist. It came near the officer's face, close enough to cause the creature to partially come out of the officer to become visible to Jonathan without having to reside in a reflection. It was hideous, clawing to scratch Jonathan, only to wind up screaming and then smash through the train window as the train pulled into the 145th street station.

Jonathan let the groggy officer down gently onto the seat, grabbed his belongings, and pulled down his hat hard over his face, and quickly but calmly exited the car when the doors opened, avoiding as many of the surveillance cameras as possible.

It all happened so fast. How did it know where he was? His eyes raced rapidly back and forth, side to side, thoughts racing only to lead him into a new kind of fear, wherein anyone could be the tool of this creature. If there were the slightest sound behind him, he'd turn in a panic. "C'mon, I'm better than this! This is the second attempt on my life. Shit, maybe a third!" he mumbled as his pace quickened, rambling like an overtly nervous lunatic.

He'd have to call Blinky and Joey in the morning. The creature left him again, but for how long? The walk home had his nerves wired for fight or flight mode, with every person coming toward him as seen as a possible threat.

When he finally made it to his apartment, he quickly threw off his coat and rummaged through the pockets, taking everything out until he pulled out a small plastic bag containing Joey's "emergency kit."

There were small plastic vials of fragrant oils, candles along with a 10 oz plastic bottle of holy water, and other herbal concoctions with minor instructions for use and what prayers or sacred words or thoughts he needed to focus on in a prayer-like manner. While he ran the bath, he poured some of the holy water into a small spray bottle lying around. He separated his clothes, placed each on a hanger, then sprayed them with the sacred water. And then wrapped each in a plastic bag, tying the ends.

He then took a relaxing bath with the scented water beneath the beautiful aroma of the lit candles. He tried to be as serious-minded as possible, considering this wasn't his thing, but he had to be honest about it. It took him a while to rid himself of the images of the day.

He had fallen asleep in the tub, got up a while later, toweled, dried, and went to bed. The only dreams he had were of Cindy and the small talk that led to the short walks in the park and laughter that weaved them closer into a cloth of friends and then lovers. He remembered her kissing him warmly the way she always did when he awoke.

Chapter 7

The kiss coincided promptly with his cell phone ringing; it was Blinky.

"Hey Jon, I didn't wake you, did I?"

"It's all good; I needed to get up anyway. How are you doing?"

"How I'm doing? How the hell are you doing? Joey told me what happened last with Henderson. Since when does he have jurisdiction over this area in Harlem?"

"You've known that man for almost as long as I have. Ever since we knew him as 'Mark, the Mechanic,' he's always been working on a deal if there's an arrangement to be made, he'll make it. He's always had the type of driving ambition that has had him crawling and climbing on the backs of anyone he could climb on to scramble up the ladder of his 'success.'"

"Yeah, I guess you're right about that."

Jonathan paused, wanting to be delicate when it came to be stepping into Blinky's personal life, "So, err, from the body language I picked up last night, were Mark and Joey an item back in the day? My bad if I'm wrong."

"Nah, you pretty much got that right. Way back in the day, when she came to New York from Chicago to attend medical school for her RN, they met. She told me about him, always on his 'stairway to heaven' groove as a means for making a name for himself. Forever on the vertical movement, he was never much for gradual inclines and always at the cost of others along the way. She was one of them, loving her for position's sake only. At least that's part of the story that leaked out when we first started dating; Henderson's in the 'let's not talk about that asshole again' place. I think her having success in her career was a little too much for him. If anyone was to set goals and grow in them, it had to be him.

"Sad to say, he's still carrying the same baggage he carried in his childhood," Jonathan added.

"Forget him!" Blinky said, "Tell me what happened to you after you left us and got taken downtown?"

"Is it okay if I come over and talk? I got a lot to talk about, and thank Joey for the 'emergency kit; it came in handy,"

"You can thank her yourself; she'll be in from the night shift at the hospital in about half an hour."

"Great, I'll be over around then."

Jonathan was about to enter the Dunbar project when he saw Joey coming up the avenue. He then had that "yes" reaction where he recognized her even more as one of the conventional fixtures/characters in the neighborhood. It was true that he had accepted her from the hospital environment but wasn't quite sure of her niche in the daily affairs of the common folk, never making the connection between the hospital and the streets. They both unfolded a bright smile at each other; she probably was undergoing the same type of reaction and lightbulb effect at seeing him.

They embraced each other with an "oh, so it's you" kind of hug, and afterward, she looked at him, asking, "What?"

"I'll tell you after we get inside."

Blinky had some fresh coffee brewing for them when they came in. Jonathan could smell the enticing aroma as he removed his shoes

"Bless you Blinky," he said as he came in watching him kiss Joey and handing both a mug.

"Thanks, babe," Joey said.

Blinky lead Jonathan into the living room while Joey went to change out of her nurse's uniform. When she came back in, Jonathan went into every detail of the evening before when he left their apartment. He included Henderson's behavior at the mention of Joey's name, the death of the captain of the freight ship and, of course, the incident in the subway car.

The tale had blown them for a loop.

"So, you're saying that you saw it partially manifest and become somewhat solid in our realm?" Blinky sounded troubled and slowly sat back on the couch.

"Yeah, I saw it, and it was hideous, like something that might have come from the deepest, darkest unknown part of our world's ocean or another world altogether, again if it wasn't for this bracelet. Do you think it's learning to come into our world?" his voice was getting stressed.

"Well, to be honest, I don't know." Blinky could see that it wasn't the answer Jonathan wanted to hear,

A quiet brooding grew between them as they finished drinking up their coffee. The silence bounced back and forth between them. Finally, Blinky leaned forward looking at Jonathan, "Just because you saw him manifest doesn't mean he's learning how to do so in our world. It could also mean that you're learning how to see him as he appears in his world. In either case, time is of the essence, and we have little time to figure this out if we're going to help you at all in this."

"Now, just how could I be learning to 'see' him?"

"All of us are capable of being sensitive to the world of spirits or realms around or connected to us in some form or fashion," said Joey. "It's quite possible that your interaction with the creature and the fact that it has had extreme physical contact with you has somehow awakened some of your psychic abilities on some level. Each of us can be 'open' in some way. For some, it's age, others like Robert are born with it, and some, like yourself, become open through traumatic experiences, etc. I mean, look at you, from here, I can sense there are changes in your aura; you're different."

Jonathan just sat back in the chair and looked at them like they were from another planet, like from where these folks be coming from? Then finally, after a few sighs of surrender, he pushed his mug out toward them and asked, "Can I get another cup of coffee?"

Blinky snickered while Joey got up smiling and shaking her head to take his mug, "Sure, you dumb ox."

"What? Did I say something wrong?" Jonathan looked bewildered.

"Nah, it's just your way. No wonder Captain Henderson loves you," Blinky added sarcastically.

Joey stuck her head back into the room and asked, "Babe, you want any more?"

"No thanks, I'm good."

Joey sashayed back into the room with Jonathan's mug. "I don't want applause, but this little lady," she pointed her finger at herself, "made some phone calls earlier today, during my break. I called the Brazilian embassy and dropped a dime on your Mr. Angler of the Lieberman Shipping and Exports Company that some cultural artifacts from the Amazon rainforest appeared to have been stolen out of their country. They needed to have their Customs Administration look into it. They said they would.

"I guess they'll contact U.S. Customs and have it looked into it." She sat down, looking at them.

Neither Blinky nor Jonathan said anything. They just looked at her and exchanged glances with each other.

She started to feel a little uncomfortable about her statement, "Did I do something wrong? Tell me!"

Blinky sat back and motioned to Jonathan to take the lead on this, obviously wanting to keep the peace with his mate.

Jonathan thought about it and then considered how to tailor his response with some diplomacy, "Hmm, actually, it may turn out that dime you dropped may cost us more than expected. I'm not saying that it didn't need doing because it's obvious we can't take the idol back to Brazil. I'm just wondering if you seasoned the brew a little too soon. I'm mean; we know what's going on with this creature, the three of us in this room. Do we want to throw more people into the mix? It's a dicer slicer, and they would be walking into this mess with blinders on."

"Okay, I see your point," she said, "Still, I feel they needed a contact in Brazil, and considering the way the wheels of this and most governments turn, they'll be the tortoise crossing the road."

"Well, we can only hope." Blinky added, "But it pushes up our time frame in dealing with this, just in case that thing is learning to manifest in this realm."

Jonathan got up to leave, picking up his coat and then remembering something in his pocket. He reached in and brought out the small spray vial with holy water he had put together earlier. "What do you think of this? I put some of the Holy Water from you're 'emergency kit,' and thanks, by the way," He referenced Joey with a nod.

"You're welcome," she said, "I had a feeling you might need it."

"Now, I don't want to sound anti-religious, but what is the deal with Holy Water? Isn't it just water that's prayed over? How can that change it to affect this creature?"

"You're not being anti-religious, Jonathan," Joey answered him; "It has to do with the power of prayer, the energy or vibration of the word, and the level or quality of one's sincerity put into it. There is more spirit to this world than people are aware of, levels of vibration for every realm in existence overlapping where maybe the most common vibes emoted is from the sincerity of heart or spirit. An object isn't dense; it's just in a vibrational state different from another vibrational state. That resonating sincerity adheres to the spiritual vibration of the object and can be felt on a subtle level. Now sometimes subtle is all you need to achieve the effect you're looking for in your prayer. Prayer should be a standard practice in blessing one's food and drink, but sadly, the more we advance technologically, the less we are aware.

"You can add a personal prayer to the water or any item, never accept it on face value, but be sincere in your need."

"Oh wow, thanks, Joey." Jonathan put the spray bottle back in his pocket. "Well, I'll see you guys later. I'm going down to meet with the artist whose name was on one of the business cards found on Simmons' body."

"I'll be at my usual spot if you want to talk," Blinky said as Jonathan departed.

Jonathan walked out of the Dunbar Projects, unaware that Detectives Louis and Rodriguez were following him.

When Jonathan reached his car, he decided to call Judith Andrew at her place of business. She was in and said she would be delighted to see him, so he got in and took off with Louis and Rodriguez following him at a reasonable distance.

Her studio was in an old artist warehouse in the Greenwich Village area of town, so he took the West Side Drive downtown.

Meanwhile, a short time later, at the J. Andrew Studio of 3-D Duplication, the doorbell rang at the studio. Two uniformed police officers introduced themselves to an attractive young woman at the door.

"Good morning," Officer Martin, "Are you, Ms. Judith Andrew?"

"Err, no, one second." She turned and called on the intercom to the back of the shop, "Judy, there are two officers at the door asking for you! Judy!" Then to the officers, "One moment, I think I see her coming:"

She finally arrived, leaving the young woman to go into the back. "Yes, how may I help you?"

Officer Evans introduced himself and his partner, "Hello, I'm Officer Evans, this is Officer Martin." He proceeded to explain their presence, "Miss, based on the Simmons' case, there may be a possible threat toward you and other people connected to this investigation. We're instructed to be outside your place of business. Another detail will be sent to your house this evening. So, we'll be outside should you need us." He pointed to the police car parked at the curb.

She was visibly distressed by the news and appeared reluctant initially but finally consented

"Err, Ms. Andrew? We're going to need to inspect the premises to check for any other access points to your facility." Officer Martin was polite but insistent.

"Oh, oh, of course," she said, inviting both officers into the reception area. "Please, don't mind the two employees working in the back, and if you don't mind, don't touch any of the artwork."

He understood and waved to acknowledge he heard her as he went through the facility.

"What do you do here?" Officer Evans asked as he waited for his partner.

"Oh, we scan with high definition laser scanners any original piece of sculptured art a client wishes to duplicate for display only. Meanwhile, it allows them to keep the genuine article in a secure storage facility.

Doesn't matter the material. We can duplicate and colorize it to the letter."

"Wow, that's pretty amazing." He remarked.

"Yes, it is." She smiled back at him.

Officer Martin was heading back up the hall toward them.

"Everything okay?" Evans asked.

Martin just smiled and pulled out his weapon, and shot Ms. Andrew in her abdomen.

She went down screaming in agony.

Martin was going to fire again when Evans pulled out his sidearm and returned fire. He was in a virtual state of shock at his partner's actions. Evans immediately grabbed Ms. Andrews and placed her behind a sofa in the reception area while taking a hit in the buttocks. Martin jumped behind the reception desk after taking a shot to the leg. They exchanged gunfire while the two screaming employees in the back started to panic..

Jonathan was walking down the street when he heard the gunfire along with other people on the block, including Detectives Louis and Rodriguez, who ran past him with their guns already drawn as Jonathan was pulling his out and cautiously approaching. He knew what it could be; they didn't. Rodriguez showed Jonathan his badge as he and Louis ran past him.

They shot and kicked in the street-level door. Jonathan was close behind them. When Louis and Rodriguez came in, they saw Martin and Evans firing at one another. Martin made the mistake of turning toward the two detectives when Evans put a bullet in his chest; he flew back dead. Ms. Andrews was still squirming on the floor in pain and bleeding out.

"Officer Evans, drop your weapon! Drop your weapon now! Place your hands on your head! Do it now!" Louis shouted.

Evans looked at him, and then with both hands on his weapon, he pointed the gun down at Ms. Andrew, preparing to discharge his weapon. Louis fired and hit Evans in the shoulder. Evans fired at Louis, hitting him in his side, leading Louis and Rodriguez to fire into Evans, who went down. Louis then turned to Rodriguez as Jonathan was coming through the open door and shoots, hitting him in the arm, forcing Rodriguez to fire back, causing Louis to slump over. Jonathan went to help Rodriguez with his wound when Rodriguez turned his gun on Jonathan, only to have Jonathan spray him the face with Holy Water. The creature came out of Rodriguez screaming, pushing Jonathan out of the way as it slammed into the parked police car, leaving a sizable dent. It went screaming down the street; people turned to see where the sound came from, but no one could see it.

Police cars with sirens blaring came streaming down from everywhere in the neighborhood. Someone on the premises had notified the police. Jonathan took off his coat, rolled it up, and moved quickly over to Ms. Andrew, placing it under her head. He then called for one of her employees to bring whatever first aid kit they could find. The young woman who answered the door brought out a first-aid kit, but she was shaking hysterically. Her whole body trembled.

When she put the kit down by Jonathan, he could see she needed to calm down, but he didn't have the time to wait for her to achieve it. He grabbed her arms and calmly but sternly told her, "Listen! I said, listen! Do you know where you are? Hello? I said, do you know where you're at?"

She nodded her sobbing and wiping her eyes.

"I need you to hold his large pad on the spot where she's bleeding and apply pressure until EMS gets here! Do you understand?"

Again, she just nodded. Jonathan grabbed her hand, placed it on Ms. Andrew's wound. "Keep pressing it; I need to look at the other wounded officer. A young man came out from the back, and even though he was a bit shaken as well, he told Jonathan he would help her.

Jonathan took the kit over to Detective Rodriguez, who was slowly regaining consciousness. "What the fuck happened?"

"Where are you hit?" Jonathan asked.

"In my arm, it went through, just gauze me up, I'll be alright." Rodriguez came to realize what he had done, saw his partner dead, had tears in his eyes, "Why did Louis shoot me? For God's sake, why?"

Jonathan padded him on the shoulder to comfort him, then went back over to Ms. Andrew and her employees, "How is she doing?"

"She passed out, but she's still breathing."

"Quick question, did Ms. Andrew do any work for a Mr. Simmons or a Mr. Angler?

The young girl, who was finally able to calm down, said, "Yes, yes, a Mr. Angler brought an old wooden sculpture in that was about three feet in height a week or so ago. He said a Mr. Simmons recommended us to him."

"So, what happened?"

"We made an exact copy, just as we always do; it was a perfect match except it weighed less."

"Did Mr. Angler pick it up?"

"No, his son came by to pick it up." She was starting to get the shakes again as tears began to flow down her face freely. He figured that was enough questioning for now.

It was just a few moments later when other police in SWAT tactical gear came storming in with weapons drawn.

Jonathan put his hands up immediately while a few of the team went through the building, yelling and repeating, "Clear!"

Paramedics followed them in and took Ms. Andrew into their care while going over to check the fallen officers.

Jonathan got up and looked outside the shattered pane glass window to see a crowd gathering and Detectives Matthews, Samuels, and Captain Henderson rushing down the block from the corner. He felt a wave of uncomfortableness pass through him and just prepped himself for the bad vibes that were about to go down.

Officers from other districts and EMS crews, and crime scene units were all busy in the space. Matthews and Samuels came in as Captain Henderson talked to Detective Rodrigues, being attended to by paramedics.

Matthews came over to Jonathan, "What the hell are you doing here? Didn't you get my message that Henderson had a tail on you?"

Jonathan shook his head; once again, he didn't check his phone as he should've. He raised his hand to Matthews in an 'I got this' manner.

Samuels came over and asked Jonathan, "Hey man, how did you know about this place?"

"That's exactly what I want to know." Henderson was doing his best not to lose his cool in the presence of other officers from other areas of the city. To Jonathan, he always looked too tight-fitted in his clothes. It was like there was no way in hell that Henderson could be loose or comfortable with people.

"Well, Mr. Simmons' brother had asked me to look into his brother's death, and I told him I would pro bono. Somewhere in our conversation, the name of Simmons' boss, a Mr. Angler, and Ms. Andrew came up. So, I just took a hunch and decided to come down here and talk with the woman. The last thing I expected was for this to happen. Ask your detective over there. He and his partner ran into the building just ahead of me."

Samuels went over to the detective, talked to him for a few seconds, and returned.

"Detective Rodrigues confirms your story," Samuels told Henderson, who nodded his head in approval. Henderson turned to Jonathan, "Just see me before you leave; I have to talk to some of the officials around here."

Henderson walked away to speak to someone. Matthews looked at Jonathan, gave a nod, and winked him a 'thank you.'

* * *

It took them quite a while going about their business of even coming close to a conclusion of what happened. Still, toward the end of the process, Henderson came back to talk with Jonathan, who was leaning against the brick wall in the reception area, talking to other officers from other precincts who might've recognized him.

Henderson caught Jonathan's attention and motioned for him to join him in the corner of the room, out of earshot of others still on the scene. He never understood the level of respect Jonathan could achieve with other officers just by being who he was. In truth, Henderson was jealous of Jonathan's natural flow of character and personality.

Jonathan wasn't quite sure what Henderson wanted to say to him when he came over. Henderson reached out to grab him and guided him further into the corner.

"What's up, Capt.?" He could see by the look in his eyes that Henderson was on a low boil. Having just lost three officers was probably the reason behind it.

Henderson looked at him, cold and hard, starting the dialogue slow and deliberate, "Tell me one thing, just one thing Mr. Hood! Why are you so Goddamn lucky? It should've been your ass lying on the floor, not Detective Louis. What is it that makes you impervious to harm?"

"I don't understand what you're talking about, Capt." He had never expected to hear this side of Henderson; this was something different.

"You don't see it, do you?" Years ago, your partner, Chris Kingston, and now these officers, your client Mr.

Simmons, the ship captain, and here Ms. Andrew, who is now clinging to life, and yeah, don't let me forget your wife Cindy driving in a tampered car meant for you."

"What did you say?" Jonathan flashed a rage Henderson hadn't seen since Jonathan broke his nose years ago. Jonathan clenched his fists and moved closer to Henderson.

Henderson put a little more distance between them as some of the officers nearby started looking in their direction.

"What the hell are you talking about? Are you losing your fucking mind?" Jonathan fumed, doing his best to keep his voice down.

"Alright, alright, I didn't mean to have it sound the way it did. It just came out wrong. I've just lost three officers, three fine officers who turned on each other. I'm a little stressed out. This shooting looks bad, bad for me, bad for the department."

So, it looks bad, bad for you, Jonathan thought, *it's always about you.* "So, what is it now? Are you blaming their deaths on me? Now it's my fault that they shot themselves?" Jonathan came back at him.

"Look, you've always been able to get out of scrapes; ever since I've known you since our growing up together, you get positions with little ease, while I had to work hard to get what I want."

"Bullshit! I don't know what you got up your ass right now but forget about working hard. If this bothers you, then it should, but you can't blame it on anyone, and you can't sweep it under the rug like every other shit that's gone wrong. Yeah, this may very well put a damn crack in that "ladder of success" of yours, but sooner or later, the dirt you try to sweep under the rug becomes part of your bathwater!"

"What are you talking about?"

"You want to blame me and my luck when talking about my partner or my wife! You know as well as I do that Syd Barnes was behind their deaths. As a matter of fact, I gave you enough evidence to nail Barnes to the wall and keep his ass in prison, remember? But he gets out on a technicality! Did you ever turn it over to the prosecutor? What happened to the evidence? Huh?"

Jonathan continued, "It was on that day you were all prettied up to go kiss some ass at a mayoral affair at City Hall so that you could move up that damn social ladder of yours, and you want to talk about luck. I don't have to explain shit to you."

Jonathan backed away from Henderson, figuring he better put some space between him and Mark before being arrested for assault on a police officer. "Listen, you're not my boss, and besides, I wouldn't answer you if I could. On the day you earn my respect, you'll be the first to know."

He turned and started walking away, saying to Henderson, but now caring if others heard, "I bet you the evidence I gave you on Barnes is still buried somewhere in your desk."

Jonathan had had enough and was about to leave when Samuels came up to him and grabbed his right arm and shouted to Henderson, "Hey Capt., look!"

Samuels pointed at a hardly recognizable. Micro-surveillance cameras in the corner of the ceiling.

101

Henderson, in turn, called to Matthews and others and pointed to the camera as Samuels had done. He turned to the young man who worked in the place and was waiting for the police to leave to close the shop.

He asked him, still pointing, "Young man, were those cameras on during the shooting?"

"Err, yes, sir."

"Can we view the recording?"

"Sure."

Henderson regained his composure and referred to Jonathan in his official captain's voice, "Mr. Hood, don't leave just yet. I want you to see this."

About seven officers, including Jonathan, accompanied the young man to a back room. They gathered around the young man as he rewound the video, reaching the point where it showed the arrival of Officers Martin and Evans greeted by the secretary. They continued watching as Martin went off the screen in the reception area to perform his routine inspection. They watch as Martin returns after a short period approaching Ms. Andrew and his partner, only to take out his gun and fire the weapon at Ms. Andrew, hitting her in the stomach.

Right after she went down, the recording went haywire, grainy with a significant amount of static. Now and then, there were minute instances of gunfire with strange noises and sounds coming from it. Everything suddenly went black until it showed Jonathan checking Detective Rodriguez at the door opening and then rushing to Ms. Andrew.

"What the hell was that?" Captain Henderson blared, "We can't make heads or tails of what went on other than Officer Martin shooting Ms. Andrew."

He looked at the young man, "What happened?"

Perspiration was beginning to bead on the young man's forehead, "Err, I don't know, this has never happened before. It's bizarre!"

"Weird, my ass! Fix it! And what's that freaking crazy growling in the background?"

The young man pointed to the screen that was divided into four sections; he showed it to everyone in the room, "Sir, these two, where the static is taking place, are from the front two cameras, but the other two cameras showing images of the back rooms are working fine. It seems to clear up with the arrival of that gentleman there." He said, pointing at Jonathan.

"Hmm, now why doesn't that surprise me?" Henderson said, grinding his teeth together and sneering at Jonathan. He then pulled out his cell and notified the office to put two more cops on patrol near Mr. Sierra, "Yes, the antique dealer/appraiser."

Jonathan asked, "Mr. Sierra?" acting as he had never heard the name before.

Henderson finally opened up a little; at this point, he didn't know who or what he was dealing with, "Yes, another person whose name was on one of the business cards found on Simmons' body."

"Oh, like my card, and yet you didn't put offices to protect me, hmm!"

"You can handle yourself, Jonathan; you always have. Besides, Rodrigues and Louis had your back." Henderson assured him.

"Really?" Jonathan answered sarcastically, knowing full well Henderson was lying to him. "Can I go now?" he asked, getting tired of the bullshit.

Henderson heard him, but first, he wanted to confirm with the young man, "Can you provide a copy of the footage for my office?"

"Sure, yes, sir."

He turned back to Jonathan, "Yeah, yeah, you can go." He said, waving him off.

As Jonathan walked out, he muttered under his breath, "Dumbass mother—!" he reached his car, in a block crowded with city vehicles, so he had to sit and wait until the street cleared. He sat there thinking if he had not been part of what just happened, Jonathan would've never believed it, knowing what he knows.

Just sitting there in his car was beginning to wear on him. He looked in his glove compartment and decided to light up one of his cigars in "storage" there. It was another promise he made to himself to cut back on, and it was one of those "once in a blue moon" habits. He made the resolve years ago never to smoke a cigar at its entire length, so he cut it almost in half and cut the tip. It had become more of a tradition through the years, somewhat of a compromise to himself and Cindy, who wanted him to denounce the habit altogether.

He opened his car door and quietly guttered the other half of the cigar. He leaned back and took a few puffs, trying to relax as the street slowly cleared. It looked like he might be able to make it through, and he went for his keys only to jump in his seat after being startled by the ring of his cell phone. In a weird moment of guilt, as if Cindy was watching him, he found himself putting out his cigar

He pulled the cell out only to see that the number on display was from an unknown caller.

"Hello? J. Hood is speaking."

"Mr. Hood, hello, this is Gloria Singleton, Samantha's friend."

"Oh, yes. How is Samantha doing?"

"I'm sorry, but I didn't know who else to call. I'm not even sure if I should be calling you about this, but I had to call someone." She sounded frightened and on edge.

"Is everything okay? What's up? You sound upset."

"It's Samantha; there's something peculiar going on with her. Symbols are rising just underneath the surface of her skin. She appears to be going in and out of a trance or something every so often. I'm anxious."

He asked her for her address and found out from Gloria that Samantha was currently sleeping. He told her that he needed to contact someone and see if they could come with him but that he would be there as soon as possible.

He knew, or at the very least, he felt he needed to contact Joey. He knew that she would probably be asleep, so he figured he better call her and give her a heads up.

The phone rang for a while before he got a tired voice asking who it was.

He immediately apologized and explained the situation to Joey and that he would pick her up.

She was able to stir and sit up and ask where they had to go.

"Brooklyn."

105

"Well, as long as I can sleep along the way, come on and pick me up, but call her friend and have her bring over a priest. People accept healing from things they accept, and it's not for me to go against their beliefs. I'll need to bathe properly, so don't rush getting up here. Understand?"

"Yes, thank you. See you later." He said, hanging up.

He called Gloria back and told her to secure a priest if possible; he would be there soon. She indicated that it might prove difficult, but Jonathan told her to make it happen as Samantha's life may be at stake. He knew she didn't particularly care to do it, but her needs really didn't matter, not if she wanted his help and wanted to help Samantha.

He looked ahead, and there was space in the street for him to get by now, so he slowly pulled off, passing by to see Captain Henderson coming out of the door with Matthews, Samuels, and others. He tipped his hat to them.

Henderson grunted when he saw him, then Henderson noticed a significant dent on the side of Officer Evans' parked police car. It looked like an angry bull had rammed into it. Henderson pointed at it. Matthews, Samuels, and others had no idea what made it.

Chapter 8

Jonathan did as Joey asked and took his time getting back to Harlem; he saw her waiting at the Dunbar archway in her whites, but not her nursing uniform. Blinky was there, but he seemed to be there to guard the space around her by keeping a few feet away from her, and when anyone he disapproved of appeared to be drawing too near to Joey, he would intercept them as a beggar trying to sell sage incense, veering them off. Jonathan pulled up and motioned her to get in; Joey 'opened' the way for her.

She recognized him and climbed in the back seat after Blinky sprinkled some sage petals and blew sage smoke in Jonathan's car; she carried a cloth bag and an ornately carved cane, looking beautiful in a powerful way. There was a consuming fragrance that she gave off. Jonathan noticed it but realized it would be something she would probably need in her line of work, considering where they were going.

She quietly looked at Jonathan, who was doing his best to tolerate the sage smoke. Blinky blew her a kiss and gave her a high sign.

She returned the kiss and said to Jonathan in a voice that was more authoritative than her normal voice, "You can open your windows now. So, your car is silver, hmm, appropriate energy for you, I guess."

"Yeah, I call her the Si—"

"Shush! Not one word out of you, I need silence, and you will give me silence. Now take me to the destination and wake me when we get there. Drive safe." She leaned her head back and appeared to be in a meditative sleep. Jonathan did as she told him, there was a level of respect that her presence suddenly demanded, and he was inclined to obey.

Wow, this is a side of Joey I wouldn't want to mess with; there's no way in hell Mark Henderson could've handled a woman like her, Jonathan thought as he pulled off waving to Blinky, who returned the wave while heading back to his spot across the avenue with his cane guiding him.

Jonathan texted Gloria to let her know he was on his way. She texted, saying she had the priest from her church coming over.

This afternoon should prove interesting, Jonathan thought.

Brooklyn wasn't the Brooklyn he knew from his childhood; the flavor was more high-class sweeter. He didn't want to judge it too harshly. It had a taste that wasn't his, but it had a style. He let Joey know that they were there. She seemed to know already as her eyes were closed, but not entirely.

They went into a modern building with a doorman and a receptionist who asked them who they were there to see. Jonathan gave him his name and mentioned Gloria Singleton. Jonathan noted the receptionist was doing her best not to notice Joey in her ceremonial dress.

"Err, yes; she's expecting you. That will be apartment 11-B."

"Thank you."

Gloria, glad to see Jonathan but surprised to see Joey, invited them into a very plush apartment and introduced them to Father Bennett of the Roman Catholic Diocese as Jonathan introduced them to Joanna. His response was, in a way, more professional than what Jonathan would've expected. He greeted Joanna with little more than a raised eyebrow but gave her a warm handshake.

Suddenly from out of the backroom, a door slammed open, and Samantha stood there nude, head at a harsh angle, hair disarrayed, pointing at Father Bennett and Joey, "I want them out! Now!"

"Oh, my God!" Gloria shouted as she went to get something to cover up Samantha.

The Father sprinkled some Holy Water at her with prayer. Joey already had a rum canteen in her hand, as if she was expecting something like this to happen, and stepped forward and sprayed Samantha as she had Jonathan earlier.

Hit by the two energies, Samantha went down, shaking as in a fit. Gloria brought out a sheet from her linen closet, and the three of them covered Samantha up and brought her back to the bed she had been lying. Jonathan just stood in an unexpected trance, knowing how he would've acted as a police officer but not wanting to interfere with something held no familiarity with.

Jonathan stood at the bedroom door entrance while the three of them worked on her. Samantha was still shaking and mumbling something, and then beneath her skin, strange symbols began to surface. The priest backed off, muttering something in Latin. Still, Joey seemed empowered by her spiritual presence and the presence of an Orisha or ancestral spirit that defied the mutterings coming from Samantha, who turned to Joey only to laugh in defiance. Joey, or whatever possessed her, was unwilling to deal with this defiant attitude. And went into her bag, removed a bottle of prepared water and fragrances, and just poured it on the sheet covering Samantha as the spirit within her reprimanded the force in Samantha while wetting the bed around her. Samantha screamed out in pain and passed out, the symbols vanishing from her body.

Everyone in the room stood there silently in awe. Joey got up, shaking. She was still in possession but managed to sit in a chair and cool down through controlled breathing. Joey or the spirit in her knew everyone was carefully watching her. She waved her hand at them to let them know she was alright; it would just take a few minutes for the spirit to withdraw from being in her.

When she calmed down, she asked Gloria to hand her the bag. She took out four candles and requested that Gloria place one in each corner of the room. She apologized for having to wet her bed. She then looked at Father Bennett with a faint smile on her face and shrugged her shoulders. He smiled back, still holding his cross.

She looked at Jonathan and Gloria, "Your friend was used in a ritual or as part of one."

"What?" Gloria recoiled.

"Yes, I got images, spirit to spirit, if you don't mind me using that term."

"Gloria, I need you to prepare a bath for Samantha. It's not over yet. Whatever it was that was in her was acting like a virus from the realm of Jonathan's creature."

Both Gloria and Father Bennett looked worriedly at Jonathan.

Joey continued, "Gloria and I will wash her. Father Bennett, can you stay here?"

He nodded, not knowing exactly why she would ask him, for he had intended to do so anyway.

"When Samantha wakes up, and she will, she will need to see you, not me. Seeing me may bring her discomfort and worry. She might wonder why a woman of my spiritual nature is doing here, particularly if she has any memory of what occurred."

"I think I understand what you mean." Father Bennett responded.

She looked at Jonathan, "I brought some street clothes in my bag, don't worry, I'll make it back fine. Robert will meet me at the train station. You have work to do because we're on a tight schedule, remember?"

Father Bennett looked at Jonathan and then at Joey, trying to figure out what exactly was going on.

Joey looked at Father Bennett, "I'll tell you all about it after we get Samantha cleaned up. Actually, you may be able to help us out immensely. For now, Gloria, would you mind putting on a kettle of water for some herbal tea I brought with me. I'll leave some for Samantha to take when she is more herself."

Jonathan understood what Joey meant; he needed to see Mr. Angler. He realized that there was still

111

enough time to catch him at his office. All he needed to do was to get into mid-Manhattan. Gloria and Joey walked Samantha to the bath that Joey had prepared with fragrances and oils. He excused himself, saying goodbye to Father Bennett, who accompanied him to the door.

When both women got Samantha in the tub, Joey sang a prayer song as though Samantha were her child and she her mother.

"I don't know what it was you did but thank you! I'm happy you came with your gentleman friend." Gloria said to Joey.

"Oh, he's just a friend of my companion," Joey answered with a smile.

"Oh really, just a friend, you say?

Joey nodded and just left it there. The last thing she wanted to get into was small talk over a man, especially having been through what she had recently experienced. She would need to see if Father Bennett could help with customs through the Church in Brazil after she unfolded the actual circumstances behind the "creature" she mentioned earlier. Whether he believed her or not was up to him. She didn't look down on the Church, but her faith in the Church to accept her story was still unfounded.

Jonathan found a parking spot in midtown and walked a few blocks to the address of Lieberman Shipping and Exports. It was on the 31st floor. The elevator opened to a well-groomed, professional establishment, with carpeting, framed portraits of former and current heads of the company.

He walked over to the receptionist. She looked attractive and looked like she had put in a long day.

"Excuse me," Jonathan said.

"Yes," she did her best to put on a bright smile, "Who are you here to see?"

"Is Mr. Robert Angler in today? You can tell him a Mr. Jonathan Hood is here to see him."

Somehow the very mention of Mr. Angler's name led to a cascade of uncontrollable, nervous jitters. It was as if the man's name would be the last thing she expected to hear as she began fumbling with papers on her desk and looking for support from one of the other secretaries off to her side.

"Err, one moment, please." She finally made a phone call to an extension where she tried but failed to discreetly tell someone that a gentleman at the reception desk wanted to speak to Mr. Angler.

"Err, Mr. Hood, is it?" She asked, getting Jonathan's attention, even though he had been listening the entire time.

"Yes."

"Someone will be out to see you in a moment," she added, doing her best to look calm.

"Oh, okay."

Just then, a door opened from down the hall, and a middle-aged woman came out with files under one arm. She came directly over to Jonathan with an open hand and introduced herself as Mrs. Gwen Harper.

"Mr. Hood, I presume?"

Jonathan shook her hand, nodding.

"Mr. Angler is on sabbatical for two months. He should be back in about three weeks. If you're still interested, I can arrange an appointment," she said.

Jonathan immediately recognized the cold-shoulder treatment he was getting, but he decided to play along. He gave Mrs. Harper his private investigator business card and got the anxious look he expected.

She looked at it, "Is there something wrong, Mr. Hood?"

"I understand he recently took a trip to Brazil; I just wanted to ask him some questions about it and a question about another employee of your firm, a Mr. Scott Simmons."

"Oh, I'm so sorry to have heard about the tragic death of Mr. Simmons. I'll be sure Mr. Angler gets in touch with you as soon as he returns."

"Well, I've been hired by Mr. Simmons' brother to look into the case, so if you should hear from Mr. Angler before he returns, please have him call my number. It's right there on my card." Jonathan answered her, pointing to his card."

"Will do, Mr. Hood," she said, offering her hand in a farewell gesture. She just wanted him to go already.

Jonathan reached out and took hold of her hand and applied his winning smile, "I don't suppose you could give me Mr. Angler's home address or telephone number?"

"Oh, I'm sorry, Mr. Hood, but that's against company policy," she responded with a slight girlish blush of her own.

"Then maybe you can help me get in touch with his son?" he added as a second thought.

"Oh, you must be mistaken, Mr. Hood, Mr. Angler doesn't have any children."

"Oh, I guess I must be mistaken, thank you, Mrs. Harper." He nodded his head in respect and went back to the bank of elevators. Thinking to himself, *So Mr. Angler doesn't have a son.* Before the elevator arrived, he made a note of the men in the portraits and realized, after reading the small type, there was Mr. Robert Angler's portrait staring him in the face. A dark-haired man in his forties

"Damn, I know him. I mean I've seen him before!" he said to himself, pulling out his cell phone and taking the elevator to the street level.

It was about 4:20 in the afternoon. Jonathan reached his car and leaned against it, giving a quick search around him, just a precautionary glance to make sure the coast was clear. The way the day was, getting caught unaware could prove costly. After several tries to find the photo he wanted, he couldn't find it.

"Damn piece of shit!" he yelled at his phone. He knew it was in there, but where?

He got in his car and tried again when the thought came to him to find the email of the pictures he sent to Simmons before Simmons asked him to get off the case. It took him a bit, but when he finally found them, he blew a few of the pictures up of the man next to Samantha, and sure enough, there he was, Mr. Robert Angler.

"Damn it, Jonathan, pay better attention, you jackass!" he cursed himself, realizing he had Angler's picture on him all this time.

In one of the photos, he saw the name of the club, where Angler and Samantha stood, and he remembered

115

them going into, The Risqué Touché. He had heard of the club's notorious reputation. It was a members' only club, known for having wild sex parties, with private, personal rooms where orgies and other freakish activities would occur.

The Risqué Touché, somehow when he followed Samantha; he just discounted places like that. He figured she was just another sweet babe looking for a good time. He didn't consider that she was dating someone Simmons was acquainted with, his boss. He thought sending Scott some pictures of one of the guys she was involved with would be enough to prove she was messing around and save him some grief. Instead, what did Jonathan do? He sent Scott pictures of his wife with his boss; he could hear himself in his head mouthing the words, *Talk about an out-of-the-park home run. Shit, unbelievable!*

"I'm fuckin' unbelievable! Those photos must have really rocked his world!"

He leaned over and looked at himself in the rearview mirror of his car and asked himself, "Any other smart moves you want to show me?"

He shifted back to his seat, somewhat disappointed at his performance in the way he was handling this situation. *Maybe Henderson has a point in saying I'm just lucky,* he thought. He sat there for a quick second, "Hell no, fuck Henderson, I've just gotten sloppy, and I've been taking this job for granted, using it as an excuse for the excellent work I used to do when I was a full pledge New York Police Detective."

He needed a pep talk, and the only one that could give him one at the moment was sitting there inside of him. *Jonathan, you got this, you got this horse, and you've been riding it for years. Now get back up, get back on it, and kick some ass. You're better than this.* He shook his head and wiggled his shoulder to get that monkey off his back.

He took a few deep breaths and put out a call to Joey, but there was only a busy signal. "She must be in transit," he thought, "After all, she did say she would be heading back uptown on her own." He then called Blinky.

"Blinky?"

"Jon?"

"Yeah. Where you at? You sound weird?"

"Oh, it's probably the acoustics of this stall in Jack's Bar and Grill."

"What? Are you taking a shit?"

"Yeah!"

"Damn, want me to call you back later?"

"Nah, man, it's cool." There was the groan of a deep push and then the sweet sound of relief, "Ahh. Okay, what's up?"

After hearing a wayward chuckle on the other end of the line, Blinky asked, "Jon, you still there?"

Jonathan regained control of the mental image projected in his head. Yeah, I'm still here, are you?" and the way he put it made both of them laugh.

"Relax, Jon, the world doesn't stop spinning because a human takes a shit; we're not that important!" Blinky added.

"Yeah, yeah, I suppose you're right. Listen, Blinky, sorry to disturb you, but during the healing session with Joey and Samantha, which I must say was not only impressive but a sight to behold. Joey mentioned a term, and I hope I'm getting this right, something about a 'spiritual virus' if I'm using the term correctly."

"Yes, I talked with her before she left Samantha's friend's apartment. You're talking about a virus from another realm?"

"Yes, that was the impression she gave."

"Well, one second, Jon, let me get up and wash." There was the sound of water running and then the electric hand dryer, and then the voices of other people in the background from the bar room, "Well, as I was saying, Jon, it stands to reason that if beings and creatures can pass through, why not a virus or other small life forms. Ya think?"

"Do you think that it might have some connection with the idol?"

"It could have, or maybe to the creature that possessed Samantha has the virus. Maybe it infected her. Still, you could be right, it could be something like rabies in our world, and without knowing it, a human would go mad or develop evil tendencies that they wouldn't normally possess on their own just by touching or coming someway in contact with the piece."

"Hmm, I see what you mean," Jonathan said, being quiet with his thoughts. "So, you're saying, whoever is handling it should wear protective gear such as plastic gloves?"

"If that's where it's coming from, sure, and if not, at least fragrant scented cloth prepared for handling it."

"You think you could?"

"Already on it. When Joey gets back, we'll put something together for you."

"Thanks."

"By the way, Jon, how did your meeting go with Angler? Joey told me you left to go see him."

"He wasn't there, and his secretary was giving me the run around saying that he was on a sabbatical and couldn't be reached, you know, some kind of bullshit."

"What's your next move?"

"I'm going to head back over to Gloria's place, Samantha's friend, and have a chat with Samantha. Apparently, she and Angler were having an affair, and Mr. Angler was Scott Simmons' boss."

"Hmm, so the world does go round and round. As always, watch your back. I'll see you later; I have to meet Joey."

"Later, Blinky."

Chapter 9

Jonathan was sitting in his car for a while after speaking with Blinky. He then called Gloria and asked her how Samantha was doing after her ordeal.

"Oh God, I'm so grateful that you brought Joanna with you. She was a godsend. Samantha is doing so much better; she's nearly back to her normal, sweet self."

"Would you mind if I came over and asked her one or two questions?"

"No, I don't mind, err, you aren't planning on getting her upset, are you?"

"Oh, I hope not, but then again, maybe I can talk just to you when I get over there, and you can get answers to my questions for me, you know, in the way girlfriends talk about things. I mean, if it's okay with you."

"Well, I can try, as long as it doesn't make her upset; she's been through quite a lot today, and she's just saying goodbye to Father Bennett. What do you want me to ask her?"

"Let me ask you this first. Do you know if Samantha was seeing other men? Please be honest if you do."

"Well," she paused for a few seconds and then decided to plunge on into it, "Yes, she and Scott were having marital issues, and her interests were expanding. We used to talk about it often, and she wasn't ashamed of it, at least that's what she told me."

"Did you know she was going out with Scott's boss, Robert Angler?"

"Hmm, yes, she told me she met him a few weeks ago at an office party held by her husband's company, Samantha can be wild and adventurous, and she recently told me about this wild club Mr. Angler took her to, where there was a three-some-couple orgy. Can you believe it? That girl is something else! Err, Mr. Hood, have you ever been to an orgy?" Her tone changed dramatically, becoming somewhat aroused by the topic.

"Err, let's stay on the topic, Gloria. Now can you do two things for me?" Jonathan asked.

"Why anything for you, Mr. Hood." Her voice didn't return to normal; the passion and longing remained. Jonathan had to dismiss it as best he could.

"One, could you ask her if there was an idol or wooden sculpture in the private room she was in, and two, could you get the names of the two other couples who were in the room with her and write them down for me; this way I won't have to disturb her at all. Can you do that?" Jonathan sounded a little too serious for her to continue with her charade.

"Oh, of course, Mr. Hood, I'll do my best. I'm sorry."

"Thank you, Gloria. I'll be over shortly," he said, hanging up, starting up his car, and leaving Manhattan.

It wasn't that Jonathan didn't find her attractive; it was just that, so far, everyone involved or connected to this case was a formula for disaster, and for now, he could only trust those he could only afford to rely on, and she wasn't one of them.

When he arrived at her address, she was in the lobby waiting for him. She greeted Jonathan telling that she left Samantha resting quietly and that she gave her some herbal tea that Joanna had left behind.

The lights in the lobby came on as daylight began to wane. Jonathan brought his writing pad and asked Gloria if she had anything worthwhile to tell him, based on what he needed from Samantha.

"Well, from what I could get from Samantha was that Angler was a stud who made reservations for a private room at the club. She said that there were two other couples with them in the room. She said that it had happened a few times before, only the last time Mr. Angler had a wooden sculpture that they used as a phallic symbol throughout the session which they rubbed up against and well, you know, acting like they were worshipping it," she said, intensely looking at him.

He looked at her. *Damn, she's fine,* came the thought, only to be dismissed as quickly as it came. "What about the names of the other couples who were with them that night?"

"Well, she only remembered the names of one of the couples, the other couple she never met before, and the only thing she could remember about them was that they were an actual couple who lived together in Manhattan."

"Damn," he quietly said to himself.

"Is anything wrong?" Gloria asked.

"Err, not really, nothing I can't handle. Give me the names you have."

She handed him a folded piece of paper with the names Michael Stephens and Joyce Banister on it.

"Mind if I keep this?"

"Of course, it's okay."

"How did Samantha react to the questioning?"

"Playfully, as usual, thinking it was just girl talk." Gloria blushed.

Jonathan took her hand and kissed it before getting up to go. "You've been a big help. Call me if you need anything."

"Oh, I'll call you." She flirted.

Jonathan shyly smiled with a wink and a nod as he departed.

When he got back to his car, he went over his information. They used the sculpture as a phallic symbol in an orgy, three couples, six people, with two names besides Angler and Samantha. There were also two unknowns. He thought about quietly inviting Detective Matthews to the fray.

Jonathan figured Matthews would be getting off work about now, if not earlier. He called him, not quite sure how he could reel him into the case without telling him too much, especially should Matthews bring in Samuels. Samuels was a little too quick when it came to kissing Henderson's ass as far as Jonathan was concerned. Still, he needed the police to look into the whereabouts of the two knowns and unknown couples. He was just one man, and he realized that he couldn't be everywhere every time.

"Matthews? How you're doing?" Jonathan pulled the phone away from his face and thought about how to work his intro, "You off work?"

"Yeah, got off about an hour ago. What's up?"

"Remember you asked me to let you know if I came across anything on the Simmons case?"

"Yeah, what you got?"

"I found out that Simmons' wife Samantha was dating his boss, a Mr. Robert Angler, and they had a little affair at that sex club on the west side, the Risqué Touché."

"Yeah, I heard of it. So, what, you think this Mr. Angler guy was involved in Simmons death?"

"Anything's possible, I've learned from his office that Mr. Angler is unavailable and unreachable at the moment, but I was wondering if you could look into the names of the two other couples who were involved in the private affair?"

"By affair, I presume you mean orgy?" Matthew corrected him.

"Well, yeah."

"Alright, I'll take a look-see. Give me the names."

"Their names are Michael Stephens and Joyce Banister. I don't have the names of the other couple."

"Okay, got it. You sure this Angler fellow is out of town?" Matthews asked.

"To be honest with you, I'm not sure, but I'm looking into it further. I can give you a heads up when I find something."

"Alright, Samuels and I will follow up on this tomorrow."

"Hey, thanks, man."

"Hey man, watch your back; the captain is at a loss for words after that shooting incident," Matthews warned him.

"Yeah, I can only imagine," Jonathan answered him.

"Hey Jonathan, you wouldn't happen to know what made a huge dent in the side of Officer Evan's patrol car, would you?"

"No, I wouldn't. Why you ask?"

"Because it looks like something or someone did quite a bit of damage to it. Henderson is having some experts capture all the instances of light from that video, and they're splicing them together."

"Wow, how's that going? Jonathan asked.

"They're still working on it, but it's coming. Okay, Jonathan, I got to go now." Matthews finished.

"Matthew, before you go, what hospital did they take Ms. Andrew to?"

"Bellevue. Why?"

"Nothing special. I just wanted to ask her a few questions."

"You'll be lucky if they let you see her, but as I said, I gotta go."

"Okay, talk to you later."

Jonathan knew that sooner or later, he would have to convey to Matthews and even Henderson something of the strange truth involving this case. For now, he worried about the thought of Samantha being "infected" by coming in contact with that idol. Then all those who attended that orgy might be infected, even Mr. Angler. With no one to work on them the way Joey worked on Samantha, things just might get ugly. For now, he would only give the police a list of possible suspects and clues that would make it appear like a standard case, anything else he'd have to play by ear.

125

Before heading uptown, Jonathan made a quick stop at Bellevue Hospital and, much to his surprise, found Ms. Andrew in a room by herself, sitting up in bed watching TV with no police security around. It was near the end of visiting hours, and he realized that she was surprised to see him when he entered her room.

"Mr. Hood, wow, I didn't expect to see you!"

"I'm sorry if I upset you. I'll go if you like. Err, I just wanted to see how you were doing and ask you a question. No security?" he asked her.

"Oh no, thank you so much. If it weren't for you, I wouldn't be here. And as for the guard, he was taken off duty about an hour ago after the doctor gave me a clean bill of health. It appears the bullet didn't hit and vital organs. They're discharging me in a few days."

"That's good to hear."

"Now, what was that question you wanted to ask me?" she reminded him.

"Oh, I just wanted to know, how do you and anyone in your business handle original pieces of art?"

"It's company policy to handle all pieces with protective gloves to prevent human contact with skin and other bodily oils. Why do you ask?"

"It was just something I needed to know, thank you. It's good to see you're doing well. Listen, I'll let you get some rest; maybe we'll talk again soon. I'll be seeing you."

"Thanks for coming by," she responded with a strange what-was-that-all-about look on her face.

Jonathan felt odd as he walked back down the hospital hall back to the bank of elevators. He knew that he must've sounded weird to Ms. Andrew, but he was relieved to see that she and her workers avoided touching the piece, which would hopefully keep her and her employees free from the virus. Jonathan knew it was better to get his fears out of the way now than to have to put her and her people down as a possible risk. He only hoped the creature would leave her alone, long enough for him to get the idol back to Brazil.

As it was growing late, Jonathan wanted to see if he could meet with Joey and Blinky before the night was over. He called, and Blinky answered. Joey was taking a healing bath, but it would be okay for him to come up in about an hour, so once again, he took his time heading uptown.

Jonathan was reaching that point in his life where he didn't feel like trusting anyone again. He sat there in his car, drawing his conclusions, and he came to the realization, how could he? That creature could be anywhere, at any time, in anyone. He knew he had to be careful, for he knew all too well where the "road to distrust" led. After he lost his partner and then his wife, the toll booth to self-medication opened up like a six-lane highway, and for a while, there was no stopping him.

He was beginning to regain a level of trust in Blinky and Joey. And much to his surprise, even Matthews. He didn't need to squander their efforts in helping him along with any other budding friendships that were beginning to blossom

The mere presence of the creature, at this point in his life, gave him an adrenalin rush he hadn't tasted in a long time – "fear." He accepted the fact that he was out of his league, but there was no running, no hiding from something that seemed destined to find his ass. He would have to find more folks to help him, even those who claimed a strong dislike for him. If it meant surrendering his ego for a while, then so be it.

When he arrived in Harlem, he cautiously got out of his car, took a quick 360° survey of the area around him, checked his revolver, and walked over to the Dunbar Projects.

Joey greeted him at the door with a kiss on the cheek and a hot cup of coffee.

"Anything stronger?" he asked.

"Try stirring it," she smiled.

He stirred and took a sip, "Vodka?"

She smiled with a shrug of her shoulders.

"Interesting," he said, waving to Blinky, who was watching them from a seat in the living room. After putting on his slippers, he walked into the living room, placed his cup on a coffee table, and plopped himself onto the sofa.

"What a day!" each word coming out of him had its own drum roll and curtain call.

Joey came in and sat next to Blinky, "I won't argue with you there," she confessed.

Jonathan took another sip and, noticing the slight buildup of silence between them, he decided to break it with a question to Joey, "So what did you say to Father Bennett? Did you have to convince him of what we might be dealing with?"

"There was no convincing necessary; he knew very well what he experienced and that we were dealing with, something the 'Church' would rather dismiss or deny publicly. He said that he would contact the Brazilian authorities. And would have officials talk to the tour guide who handled Mr. Angler's tour to find out the region of the Amazon he explored and hopefully bring back one or two shamans to the United States to handle the piece."

"Do you mind me asking what it was that you picked up about the virus in Samantha?" Jonathan was curious, but he didn't want to step on anybody's toes.

Joey, however, didn't seem to mind, "Well, while we recognized that something was possessing her, my spirit guide, if you will, recognized it as something different from the normal spiritual possession that I've been accustomed to experiencing."

She leaned forward and looked at Jonathan truthfully; she continued, "It was enough to pick up on what was affecting her. It's just a feeling that comes through when one, like me, stops being the driver in their vessel and becomes a passenger. I envision things as a bystander." She paused, adjusting her seating position and clearing her throat before moving on. "It's a little hard to explain unless one has experienced it, considering all the imagery and all the flashes firing through one's mind, but it becomes part of one's perception as it became part of mine."

She sat there quietly looking at Jonathan, knowing all too well he didn't know a damn thing about the topic of discussion. He looked at her knowing she knew, and started to say something when she added simply,

"Jonathan if I knew how it works, it would probably be common knowledge available to every one of us. It's a perception, and it was what I sensed from experience."

He sat back and just nodded. He realized that he had asked enough concerning the subject.

Blinky felt the need to interject something into the conversation, seeing how Jonathan was fumbling the ball, "When you called me earlier Jonathan, you mention that they used the idol as a phallic symbol in an orgy at a sex club. What else have you found?"

"Oh, that reminds me. No, not the phallic symbol. I'm referring to the idol." He could see he needed to clear things up a little after seeing that both of them were giving him a strange look, "Ms. Andrew and her crew never had actual physical contact with the idol as they are required to wear protective gloves and garments."

"Well, that's good to hear," Joey commented, sounding somewhat relieved.

"And as for the idol, it was taken to a sex club, the Risqué Touché, there were six people at the 'party,' if you want to call it that," Jonathan said, responding Blinky's earlier question.

"Yes, Robert told me about it when I came home. Some people, it's crazy out there," Joey added.

"Well, I was able to get the names of one of the couples who were there and who had contact with the idol. I'm having Detectives Matthews and Samuels looking into it."

"How were you able to get the names of the couple?" Joey asked.

"I had Gloria talk to Samantha and get for me, but she could only get me the names of one couple," Jonathan answered her.

"Gloria, really?" Joey asked, smiling.

"And?" said Jonathan responding to Joey's tone, blushing slightly and taking another sip as if to mask his smile and the look in his eyes. Still, Joey was smiling.

"Not you?" he laughed, putting the cup down.

"Not you, what?" Blinky's voice sounded off, placing himself in the middle of their exchange.

"Nothing!" Jonathan said, halting Blinky's inquiry.

Blinky's blinking went through a quick flurry of his eyelids, causing Joey and Jonathan to burst into laughter.

After sitting up and recovering from laughing too hard, Joey said, "It's really nothing Hon, I just think Gloria has the hots for Jonathan."

"Oh, really?" said Blinky.

Jonathan waved him off and decided it was a decent time to head home as it appeared nothing else would get done tonight. He appreciated Joey's attempt to lighten the mood, and he felt he better leave while he was laughing and feeling up.

He got up to go and shook Blinky's hand while hugging Joey and receiving a bag of bath oils from her and other essentials.

The day was reaching its end as he stepped outside, and there was a wicked wind lashing out a chill that searched for weak points in his clothing. He needed the warmth of his apartment as soon as possible.

Chapter 10

Samuels arrived at the precinct to find Matthews at his computer researching the names that Jonathan had given him the night before. He sat down at his desk across from Matthews, "What brings you in so early?"

"Hood gave me some names to follow up on." Matthews looked intensely involved.

"What names?"

"Names of folks connected to the Simmons case."

"Man, let that loser go, won't you? There's little to nothing that 'has been' can help us with." Samuels scarfed.

Matthews didn't pay him any mind but continued with his search.

Samuels started to repeat himself when Matthews held up his hand for him to stop, "Well, I'll be damned, look at this." He grabbed his pad and showed Samuels the name on his it and then turned his computer screen around for Samuels to see the same name on the computer screen. Michael Stephens, a 36-year-old male, arrived DOA to New York-Presbyterian 12:37 am from Christopher Street Downtown Station after pushing two people onto subway tracks and publicly exposing himself. Fallen pedestrians secured themselves to safety, but patrol officers in pursuit of the assailant could not apprehend the perpetrator. Because he discarded his apparel as he ran screaming, tossing pieces at officers in the chase before said assailant, Michael Stephens, ran to the end of the platform and threw himself in front of an inbound #9 train.

Samuels referred back to Matthews' pad and said, "Wow, now that's a freakin' weird coincidence!"

Samuels, whose interest was now peaked, got on his computer and searched for Joyce Banister, the other name on Matthews' pad. Matthews continued taking notes on the Stephens' report on his screen. The only thing that came upon was Ms. Bannister's photo and address with a few priors; she lived somewhere near midtown. He printed out her information, and he and Matthews got up to go pay her a visit.

As they got up and Samuels went to the printer, a bulletin flashed on the precinct's central viewing screen reporting about a woman in midtown chewing on the ear of a defenseless child she had just bitten off and biting the faces of other children. She was reportedly subdued, putting up a fierce struggle with arresting officers who took her to Bellevue Hospital Psychiatric ward. The name Joyce Banister came up with her photo.

Matthews turned by to look at Samuels' screen, "That's her! Samuels, what the hell is going on? What has Hood gotten us into?"

Samuels just looked at him, not knowing what to say.

Matthews grabbed his suit jacket, picked up his pad, and motioned Samuels to follow him.

"Where're we going?" Samuels asked him.

"To the Risqué Touché," Matthews told him.

"What the hell for?"

"To add two more names to this list," Matthews said, showing him the pad.

"Two others, who?" Samuels asked.

"I'll tell you on the way."

As they rushed out, Captain Henderson came in through the doors. "Where're you guys off to in such a rush?"

Matthews told Samuels to warm up the car and that he would be right there.

"Captain, we're following a lead from Hood, and as crazy as it sounds, this Simmons Case is turning weird in a bad way, and I mean a very bad way!"

"Okay, do what you got to do, just keep me abreast of everything that's going on."

"Yes, sir."

Matthews and Samuels went over to the Risqué Touché and were let in by the cleaning crew who were preparing the space for the events of the following evening. They had to wait for the owner/manager, who didn't arrive until around 10:30 in the morning.

They inquired about viewing the guest list of a few weeks prior, on the night that would indicate the night that a club member by the name of Mr. Robert Angler made reservations. The owner didn't want to give them the time of day, much less the names of his clientele. Matthews finally convinced him by letting him know that he could either show them the books or the club could lose a good stream of business for the next few days, if not longer.

They found the names of the unknown couple listed under a Mr. R. Angler, a Samantha Reid, Matthews and Samuels took it to possibly Samantha Simmons' maiden name; they saw an Arthur Madden and a Karen Daniels followed by Michael's and Joyce's names.

Samuels went back to his car and looked up Madden's name while Matthews finished up with the club's owner. Samuels called back to Matthews, who was coming out of the door of the club, "I've got a Chelsea address, near the West Side, Matthews jumped in, and they took off.

The address took them to a four-story tenement complex, where they got out and rang the bell, but they got no response, leaving Samuels to check the side basement entrance where he met the super who was in the back sorting the garbage.

The super agreed to open the apartment up for them. The super was a short, talkative man in his mid-fifties sporting a short but a full white beard. He went on about how he hadn't heard from them in a couple of days, "They might be out of town, you know these young people today, always on the go, traveling here, there, chasing a dream or chasing something, if you know what I mean," he chuckled, winking at them. He went on talking as they walked up the flight of stairs, "I hope this is not about them smoking weed all the time. You know they own the entire floor. At one time, it was two apartments, but they had them connected about two years ago; they must be pretty wealthy, huh?"

Maybe the super was nervous in the presence of police officers, or perhaps he was just a talker by nature, but he just kept going, on and on, "Sometimes the only way to know they're home is the burning fumes of marihuana on their floor." He let out a quick grouping of chuckles as he pulled out his keys in readiness.

By the time they all got to the fourth floor, the odor wasn't one of smoked weed, but there was the settling odor of rotting flesh. The super looked at Matthews and Samuels with alarm on his face.

Matthews just said to him, "Open the door and step back, do not come in. Understand?" He and Samuels drew their weapons.

The talkative super was now a nervous wreck, shaking the keys as he tried to open the door. Matthews had to take the keys out of his hand and open the door. The odor hit them hard, causing the super to puke on the spot, forcing him to scurry to the rooftop and prop the door open to let in some air and let out the smell.

The apartment hallway was dark with garbage strewn all over the place, and the afternoon light was slithering past fully drawn shut curtains. Samuels went over to raise a curtain and open a window. As the light rushed into the room, there on the couch was the body of a young man. His throat slit and three large knives protruded out of his chest. His look was one of shock, and he was still holding a writing book, possibly a diary, in one hand. Matthews went over to get a better look and was about to holster his weapon when a sound crept out from an adjacent room. He held on to his gun and motioned for Samuels to follow him as quietly as possible.

As they drew closer to a shut door, they could hear a woman giggling and humming a children's nursery rhyme. They edged their way over the debris of papers, broken furniture, and shattered dishes. When Matthews cautiously opened the door, the room was as dark as the hallway when they first came in. They had to readjust their eyes to the dimness of the room. Matthews almost slipped, stepping on the body of a dead, partially eaten cat beneath a piece of crumpled newspaper.

They heard a giggle and turned to see a partially nude woman with blond, crazed hair sitting on the trash-covered floor, munching on the body of a freshly killed cat. She looked at them with a wild expression in her eyes, and like a child sharing her prize with a friend, she offered Matthews the cat to feast upon as well. Its guts and inner organs still hung loosely from her mouth. Samuels stepped forward to slowly remove the cat from her hands when she quickly scratched his hand, indicating she was offering the cat to Matthews. Matthews just got on his phone and called for immediate assistance.

When the emergency crew came to clear the apartment, Henderson followed in after them. He stood off to one side of the residence while crime-scene officers took photos, allowing the removal of the man's body. Matthews and Samuels worked their way over to where Henderson was standing. Shortly later, EMS took the woman out. It was one strange scene between her giggling, humming, and occasional growl, even for someone with their years on the job.

Matthews looked at Henderson shaking his head, "Read this, sir. Apparently, it's a diary that the young man kept. The final pages tell a strange story if you ask me, so please don't ask me." He handed it to Henderson already opened on the last entry:

> *Karen's been acting strange. She's not herself and hasn't been so for the past few days; I don't know why. I know she's usually wild and giddy, but since a day or so after a romp at the Risqué Touché, she started showing a boost in her sexual drives and appetites.*
>
> *Now she's moody, hasn't said a thing or at least only mumbling to herself and watching me like some caged animal. Our cats even react to her differently. I know the only thing different about our last orgy was the weird-looking idol Robert brought. He claimed it was from the Brazilian jungle. Everyone was having fun rubbing up against it, licking it like some big penis. Personally, I refused to touch something made by some damn savages from a fuckin' jungle.*
>
> *I've got to keep my eye on her; maybe she'll come around. I g—*

It ended with blood splattered the rest of the page.

"How did you come by this place and who is this Robert he's talking about?" Henderson looked at Matthews and Samuels already impatient with them.

Samuels looked at Matthews, who confessed, "Hood gave us a lead that brought us here. And Robert is a Mr. Robert Angler, the head of Lieberman Shipping and Exports, the boss of our initial victim in the Simmons' case and one who might have been having an affair with our victim's wife; at least according to Hood."

Henderson quickly shoved the book back into Matthews' hands, raised his arms, and turned away mad as hell, "Nah, I'm not having this! No God-damn-it, I'm not having this. We're knocking on the door of the fuckin' 'Twilight Zone,' and I don't need this shit!" His yell filled the whole top floor, "I said, I don't need this shit! You promised me he might be of help in the case, and now this? Maybe you two need to be out there on the street with that fuckin' maniac! Huh? HUH?"

Samuels tried to kiss some ass by saying to Matthews, loud enough for Henderson could hear him, "See, I told you Hood was a loser."

Matthews just sneered at him.

"Not now Samuels, I don't need you to wipe my ass." Henderson slammed him.

Henderson just looked at the both of them and yelled, "Clean this shit up and meet me back the station in an hour, I need to check on our boys and that damn video and under no circumstances, and I will repeat myself, under no circumstances are you to call Mr. Hood about this. God damn —" He violently poked his finger at them and mumbled some other expletives under his breath and marched out.

Samuels' cell phone rang, and Matthews could hear him snarl to the person on the other end, "How many times have I told you not to call me on the . . ." Samuels turned to Matthews and said, "Sorry man, got to take this." Matthews gave him a nod; Samuels then headed off to the apartment's bathroom and slammed the door behind him.

Matthew picked up the muffled sounds of a turbulent conversation behind the closed door. He quickly used the time to text Jonathan, warning him that the Capt. was on the warpath and not to call and that he would contact him later. He finished up and waited when Samuels finally came out, asked him, "What, woman problems?"

"Oh yeah, damn bitch!" Samuels nervously chuckled, hoping Matthews wouldn't pry into his business any further while placing his phone back in his pocket. "Okay, let's finish up here, as the Capt. said, and let's get back to the office."

"Yeah, I guess we might as well. This is going to be bitch writing this shit up," Matthews noted, with Samuels agreeing with him.

Chapter 11

Jonathan had spent his morning tending to chores he had been neglecting over the last few days, like trying to feed an empty refrigerator that was beginning to show its wired bones. He figured he'd put a smile on his coffee pot and fire up his toaster that was nodding off underneath a package of dry-hard muffins.

He came back from the store only to realize the muffins weren't going to do it for him. He needed some breakfast. He took it upon himself to try something he hadn't done in a long time, he'd take a friend to breakfast, and Blinky was his choice. While going out the door and down the flight of stairs, he had to laugh at the notion that he hadn't had breakfast in a restaurant since a short while after he lost Cynthia.

So, he just started quietly talking to her on the way down, in the present tense, the way Blinky had suggested, "I know, I know Cindy, I've been bad. Haven't been taking care of myself the way I should. To be perfectly honest with you, I've been blaming myself for what happened to you, but then again, I quite sure you know that, and you're probably pissed off as hell at me."

He would add her into the conversation, presuming what her response would be, "Oh yeah, you are? I thought so. But what am I to do? Get over it? I'd figured you would say something like that. Tell you what, I'll work on it, but every once in a while, you'll have to forgive me if I shed a tear or two for you, babe. Yeah, it's just the way it's gonna be. Look, I'm actually making an effort to invite someone to have breakfast with me; yeah, funny, I know. So, do me a favor and give me a little credit, just a wee bit. You know I love you, yeah, I know you do too. Good morning babe, we'll talk again later."

He imagined her lips pressing against his as his eyes began to water, but somehow, he felt so much better as he walked out of the building and strolled around the corner.

The day was colder than he expected, but he didn't mind it that much.

Blinky was looking in his direction as he was coming down the street. Jonathan wasn't sure if he could see him, but when he drew near, Blinky smiled. "Got a glow about you today, what, had a nice talk with Cindy?"

Jonathan wasn't too surprised by his statement, and he wanted to give Blinky a brother hug, but he wasn't quite at that level yet. He just shook Blinky's hand and pulled him up from his seat, and said, "Breakfast or brunch, considering what time it is, is on me, come on, let's get across the street to the restaurant."

"But I . . ."

"No buts, this will be a first for you and me, so don't blow it. Yeah, and I know they may not have anything 'good' for you, but we can live it up a little for quick thirty minutes or so."

Blinky just laughed and accepted the offer, adding, "You do know I look like a blind beggar?"

"You are a blind beggar. Fuck 'em!" Jonathan laughed.

* * *

The meal went better than either one of them had expected. They joked over the food, if not about it, and rehashed old childhood and neighborhood memories, but the conversation led back to the current state of things like all roads.

Jonathan realized he hadn't spoken much about the person who claimed to be Robert Angler's son and who came to pick up the idol and its copy from Ms. Andrew's art replication company. He decided to bring it up, now that he had Blinky's ear.

"So supposedly Angler's son picked up the piece, but when you asked about his son at the office, Mr. Angler's secretary denied he ever had any children?" Blinky asked.

"That's pretty much how it went."

"Well, these days, it could be something he's keeping under the radar, like a child out of wedlock who he'd keep secret. You know anything is possible these days."

"No, I don't think he's the kind of guy who would send a son, who he wants kept secret, to go to a business and pick up something for him. No, I think there's another player in the game."

"Yeah, that sounds about right, or maybe it's someone already in the game."

Jonathan just looked at him. Blinky just shrugged his shoulders with that boyish smile he was so fond of wearing. Jonathan asked for the check and pulled out his wallet. A text message came on his phone; it was from Matthews. When he read it, it left him with a frown on his face.

"What's up?" asked Blinky, feeling the mood change.

"This may be another one of those days 'ol buddy, Henderson is on the warpath. according to Matthews. They must have found out something alarming; that would be my guess." He turned and asked the waitress for the check, telling Blinky, "Let me get you back across the street before all hell breaks loose."

As they went back across the street with Jonathan guiding Blinky, he changed his mind and said, "Blinky, you and I both know this day is going to be a mother of a day. We better have a drink together now; we may never get another chance."

"Ditto, I feel it too." Blinky agreed and then added a bad English accent, "If nothing else, but to finish breakfast 'proper.'"

"Yeah, I like that word 'proper.' Drinks are on me." He laughed, guiding Binky to their usual spot in the bar, where they ordered the usual. While musing over their drinks and looking at the bar pictures and décor, they were the picture of two cowboys, in the ol' west, watching the clock for high noon.

Suddenly Jonathan got a call from Joey.

"Hi Joey, how're you doing? No, I'm not downtown; I'm sitting right here with Robert. What's up? Father Bennett called you? One sec let me put the phone on speaker so that Robert can hear."

"Hi Babe, what's this about Father Bennett?"

"Hi Hon, he just called. He told me that he'd be meeting with Brazilian officials who will be arriving with two Amazonian shamans who are from the area where the idol once stood."

"Wow, that was quick. I thought there would be a lot more 'red tape' involved," Jonathan said.

"Apparently, the guide took them just where they needed to go. The officials found the shamans repairing and fortifying the other idol that was still standing. They were preparing a cut tree for carving to erect a new idol, but preparing it would take a full Luna cycle of rituals, etc. They're hoping if they can get the idol we have, the shamans might be able to use it as a doorstop until they complete a new piece."

"It still seems quick, though," Blinky added

"Yeah, well, he seems to know people who know people, and with the pressure from the Church to sweep this whole encounter under the rug ASAP, things happen."

"I guess you have a point," Jonathan said with Blinky approving.

"So they'll be coming in today?" Jonathan asked.

"Actually, there'll be in midday tomorrow," Joey answered him.

"Well, it's a start or a step in the right direction," Blinky said.

"We better try to get this solved; I wouldn't like the idea of having them waste a trip to the Big Apple for nothing. How do the lyrics in that song go? 'This could be the start of something big,'" Jonathan chimed in, leaving both Joey and Blinky to give a less than hearty giggle.

"Well, let's hope so," Joey yawned on her end.

"Thanks for the heads-up, Joey, and get some sleep. I know that night shift can be a killer," Jonathan sympathized

"Okay, now you guys take care of yourselves, and Honey watch yourself," she added.

"Alright, see you later, Babe," Blinky said, leaning into the phone on the table and sending a kiss.

After she hung up, Jonathan said, "Wow, she included you in my troubles. What was that about?"

"Err, she's like that sometimes, gotta love her."

They looked at each other and saw the young boy each used to be for a brief second. He and Blinky tapped them near empty glasses together to toast, "To a great day," Jonathan wished him.

"Same, all the way round," Blinky added.

"I'm gonna walk to the Silver Bullet and get her warmed up, stay close to your phone."

Blinky waved him off as he walked out. Jonathan was a little uneasy about how this day would go.

Chapter 12

"Hey, it's the 'S & M, Team.' Welcome back!" was the greeting Samuels and Matthews got from some of their fellow officers in the locker room after they had turned in their reports, as whistles blew, mixed with party shouts, high fives, and the slamming of locker doors and benches.

"Funny!" fumed Samuels, somewhat pissed off at his decision to follow Matthews into the club that led to the mess they found at the apartment downtown.

Matthews really didn't give a damn; he just hit them back by yelling at the lead instigator with, "Yeah, Sanders, just wait 'til I get your sweet, little ass at the Risqué Touché, you're mine girlie-man!" he pointed at him, moving his body in a repetitive, erotic jester. The place fell into another flood of laughter.

"Cut the crap!" It was the Desk Sargent, Matthews, Samuels; Captain Henderson wants you two in his office, pronto! He said; don't let him have to come and get you." Other officers turned to the chorus of "Oh, oh, you're in trouble now!"

"Dumb ass bunch of kids," Samuels muttered under his breath as he headed upstairs.

Henderson sat at his desk with his head in his hands. There were three reports in front of him: one for Michael Stephens, the 36-year-old male who tried to kill two innocent pedestrians at the Christopher Street station, only to throw himself in front of an inbound train. One report for Joyce Banister, 35 years old, arrested for eating a baby's ear and attacking other infants in midtown Manhattan. Taken to Bellevue Hospital, and now a third report was dealing with the arrest of Karen Daniels for the murder of Arthur Madden, a 42-year-old male. She, 38 years old, was also taken to Bellevue Hospital for observation.

They walked into his office, and he looked up at them with a tense swollen face, blood vessels all over his brow were protruding, and his eyes appeared puffed and reddened. Matthews could have sworn they looked like he was on the verge of shedding tears. They quietly sat down in front of him, it was a tense moment as they waited for the Captain to speak, and they weren't sure if he wanted them to begin the conversation. They shot glances at each other, trying to pick up on any cues Henderson might give them; finally, Matthews adjusted himself in his seat and leaned forward to clear his throat.

Henderson raised a hand for him to stop right there. In a voice struggling to control his level of anger, he said, "In an unreasonably short period, I've lost three officers, with one in the serious condition in the hospital and no explanation. Now I got to two bodies, injured pedestrians, traumatized children with wounds that may affect them for the rest of their lives, and two women literally crazed out their freakin' minds and again." He stopped, and his hands began to shake as his voice went up an emphatically high pitch, "Do you hear me? And again, there are no explanations!" He just stopped and looked at them, looking like he was about to bust out of the smaller-than-it-needed-to-be suit he was wearing.

Matthews thought it would be a good time to say something in his defense.

Again, Henderson put his hand for him to keep quiet. "Am I to understand, as in the death of my officers that somehow and in some way, Mr. Jonathan Hood was mixed up in this fiasco?" Now he sat back in his chair and looked at Matthews waiting for a response.

While nervously sitting in front of his boss, Matthews still felt pretty confident in telling Henderson about Mr. Angler and his connection with the Simmons' case involving Mr. Simmons's wife, Samantha. Actually, the longer he went on, the more relaxed he could feel Henderson getting. As he was about to go on further, Henderson's phone rang, causing him to put Matthews on hold; it was Tech Department.

"What? You were able to break down the video? Can you email me the file? Oh, you did already? Good. I'll take a look. What? You sound worried. Okay, stop the blabbering. I can't understand a word you're saying. Just let me see it. Bye!" He said, slamming down his phone, somewhat confused by the last part, the conversation. As he turned his computer to where Matthews and Samuels could see, he said, "Damn technician was dribbling on like he saw a damn ghost or something. I don't know what the hell is going on around here."

He went to his email account and logged in, and opened the file that explained the video was treated in a different spectrum of light, so they could better view the gaps in the original version. He clicked it, and it revealed a series of still shots of a translucent blob of energy hovering over Martin, the police officer who shot Ms. Andrew. It was then over Evans, the second officer after Martin laid dead. It moved from officer to officer and then to detective to detective, and then there was a still shot of Hood spraying something into the face of Rodrigues, only later to see it by the dent in the police car sitting outside the place.

"What the fuck!" was the general response of the three of them as Henderson replayed the file, slowing down the speed. Each could swear that now and again, they could depict an angry, horrid creature with seemingly demonic facial features, but not one of them wanted to admit it to the other openly.

"Call Hood," Henderson barked at Matthews.

"What?"

"I said, call Hood!" he ordered. "And put it on speaker."

Matthews did as Henderson ordered.

Hood answered the call, "What's up, Matthews?"

"Jonathan, Captain Henderson wants you to come into the station as soon as possible." He said, looking at Henderson, who didn't like the use of the phrase "as soon as possible" and had started to say something when Jonathan said, "Sure, I'll be right in as soon as I can find a parking space, I've been driving around for the last five minutes, man traffic in this part of town sucks."

They were all surprised that he was in the neighborhood. Henderson just said, "Use the police parking lot, tell them I told you to and get yourself in here!"

After a short while, Jonathan calmly walked into the office after lightly rapping on the captain's door. There was a seat waiting for him, and Henderson just pointed to it for him to sit.

Henderson was no longer in a volatile state and bluntly asked him, "How long did you know about this? He shoved the reports over toward Hood so that he could look at them, but Jonathan's expression didn't reveal much; Jonathan read it like something he would typically read. Only when Henderson played him the video file did Hood display a level of sincere uncomfortableness.

Samuels, Henderson, and Matthews sat there patiently waiting for an answer from him.

Jonathan painstakingly repeated the question to himself, "How long did I know about this?"

He put the reports back on the desk, leaned back, and let go a sigh of relief. Finally, he was just glad to get it off his chest. At this point, he couldn't give a rat's ass if they believed him or not.

He looked at Henderson and said, "I guess, truth be told, I knew about it before this whole crazy affair began."

He weighed into the story, starting when he first saw the creature in his hall mirror looking at him from outside his six-floor window. He realized later that there was a connection to it and the murder of Scott Simmons. He decided to leave out a few details in telling the story just to be on the safe side of sanity.

He began talking about the idol's origin and its ties to Mr. Robert Angler, Simmons' boss, when Henderson's phone started ringing. Henderson thought he'd just let it ring and go into voicemail, but it began ringing over and over again. Finally, there was a rap on his office door as Officer Nuñez stuck her head in, "Sir, it's Bellevue Hospital. They say it's vital that they speak with you."

Henderson appeared momentarily angry but agreed to speak with them, "Hello?"

"Is this Captain Henderson?"

"Yes. And just who am I speaking with?"

"I'm Dr. James Leonard, the Director of Bellevue's Psychiatric Ward."

"Yes, and?" Henderson said, putting the phone on speaker for the others to hear.

"Earlier today, at two different times in the day, officers brought in two patients for observation. The first was a Ms. Joyce Bannister early this morning and the second a Ms. Karen Daniels this afternoon."

"Yes, I know, now tell me, what's the problem?"

"The problem is that upon the moment each one was brought into the ward, they started screaming 'He's here, he's here!' I don't know why they would do that, but they kept yelling it until I had them sedated. It just seems highly odd, so I thought I'd notify you."

"Well, thank you," Henderson looked up, somewhat dumbfounded, not sure of what to add to Dr. Leonard's point. He saw Hood give him a hush sign while Jonathan wrote a note on a piece of paper and passed it to him. Whispering to Henderson and telling him to read it to the doctor.

"Err, Dr. Leonard," he continued reading, "Do you have a patient under your care registered under the name of Robert Angler?"

There was silence without any response whatsoever.

Henderson asked again using his authoritative voice, "I said, Dr. Leonard, do you have a patient named Robert Angler under your care?"

They could tell by the silence that the question had struck a nerve.

Henderson went at it again, "Dr. Leonard, I'm asking —"

"Yes, yes. It's supposed to be kept confidential, but yes, we do."

"When was he brought in?"

"He was brought in a few days ago. Why is there a connection?"

Jonathan gave Henderson the sign to cut the conversation short.

Henderson said, "Dr. Leonard, not to worry; we'll keep quiet about it for you. For now, keep the women sedated, and under no circumstances are they to be transferred."

"Ok."

After the call, Henderson looked at Jonathan and asked, "Why shouldn't we go there now and arrest Mr. Angler?"

"Because if he's been there for the last few days. Then someone else must be manipulating the creature; that would be my guess," Jonathan said.

Samuels leaned back and then got up and paced the room, "Man, I don't believe none of this shit. 'That would be my guess,'" he said, mocking Jonathan. "Let's just charge Mr. Angler with the Simmons murder and be done with it." He looked at Henderson, "Sorry, sir, but are we gonna let this 'Loser' tell us what to do?"

Henderson, Matthews, and Hood just looked at him and dismissed his ranting, and then Jonathan remembered his conversation with Blinky earlier.

"Wait!" Jonathan said, "What about Ms. Andrew, the video?"

'What about the video? We already saw it. And by the way, what were you spraying in Det. Rodrigues' face?" Henderson asked.

"Holy water," Jonathan answered.

"What the fuck!" cried Samuels, "And you guys think I'm nuts?"

"Which is just one reason why I never told any of you anything about this case. I would've been in a locked, padded cell alongside Angler," Jonathan snapped back.

"Okay then, what about the video?" Henderson said, trying to bring about a truce between them.

"I'm just saying, but maybe there's a video of the person who picked up the idol and the replica from Ms. Andrew's shop. He claimed to be the Angler's son," Jonathan told them.

"Does Angler have any children?" Henderson asked.

"Not that I know of, and that's exactly why we need to see if there's an available video," Jonathan pointed out.

Henderson looked through his old-style Rolodex, picked up his phone, and called Ms. Andrew's shop. Even though she was still in the hospital recovering from the gunshot wound, her shop was open. He was able to get in touch with the young man they met at the shop on the day of the shooting. Henderson asked him if he could send any photos of the man who claimed to be Mr. Angler's son and who picked up the idol.

He told him he would send it as soon as possible.

They waited as Henderson motioned Samuels to sit back in his seat, to which he complied; however, he was still on edge; Samuels felt he had other things better to do than sitting around listening to the bullshit Jonathan was spewing.

When the email pics came in, Henderson printed them out. Sadly most of the prints came out blurry, showing a young light skin young man wearing a hoody, but in two of the pics, Jonathan recognized him, "That's Carlos!"

"Carlos?" the others questioned.

"Carlos Sierra, the antiques dealer's son. You remember Francisco Sierra from Sierra's Antiques and Appraisal on 56th St. and 1st Avenue?"

Henderson nodded, stood up, unlocked his desk drawer, and pulled his revolver out to holster it. Matthews and Samuels started to rise from their seats as well.

"Wait, wait, hold on! What are you guys doing?" cried Jonathan.

"We're going over to see this Carlos Sierra, that's what," Henderson stated.

"And do what?"

"Bring his ass in," added Matthews.

"You've already lost three officers Henderson. What makes you think you won't lose more?"

"So, what are we supposed to do? Let him keep doing what he's doing?"

"At least let's think about this first, maybe come up with a plan before you go charging in." Jonathan proposed.

"Captain, really? Who died and made Hood captain?" Samuels' attitude was on fire.

"Samuels, would you shut the fuck up for once already! Damn, you're talking more than usual today. What's eating you?" Matthews shouted.

Forgetting where he was at or with whom he was with, Samuels blurted out, "I just can't stand this fuckin' uppity, smartass nigga…" then he stopped short, realizing what word just slipped from his mouth as he stared into the faces of three angry black men who were staring back at him.

"Keep that shit in the street where it belongs!" Henderson shouted, again his anger was on 'high alert,' "Because if you can't, you can take your ass out of my office and out of this precinct. Am I making myself clear?"

"Oh my God, I apologize, sir, I don't know what got into me. I just suddenly flared up! It won't ever happen again. Let me go to the bathroom and freshen up. I can see it's getting a little tense in here."

"Sorry about that, Hood," Henderson apologized for his officer's conduct.

Samuels' behavior caused Jonathan to wonder if Samuels might've, in some way, come in contact with a piece of the idol or something to that effect, but he dismissed it, accepting that Samuels might've always held a grudge against him.

Matthews put his mind to rest by saying to both Jonathan and the captain, "I've been his partner long enough to know he bends that way now and then, but personally, I don't give a fuck as long as he does his job and doesn't steer his bullshit in my direction. As for you, Jonathan, he's always had in for you, you smartass, uppity …."

The three of them busted out in laughter, easing some of the tension still lingering in the room.

Jonathan then realized Blinky's statement about Evil being on any plane of existence, being 'homegrown.'

It didn't have to come from somewhere else. Humans were quite capable of making their own brand of Evil. He looked at Henderson, who appeared nervous about the incident, and he wondered if his apology was sincere or protocol, but he didn't have time to think about it. His mind was on Carlos. He was trying to figure out how Carlos knew so much about the idol and Mr. Angler to even forge his ID enough to get away with being accepted as Angler's son.

"So, what do we need to do?" Henderson asked Jonathan, breaking his train of thought.

"Well, first, you'll need to give everybody involved rubber gloves with instructions that they are not to touch the idol or let it brush up against uncovered skin. Otherwise, they'll wind up like our folks in Bellevue."

"That should be simple enough," Henderson said.

"Second, I'd like to be allowed to bring in someone who can actually see that creature."

"What the hell are you talking about, Jonathan? And who in the hell can do that?" Henderson asked, with Matthews looking at him strangely.

"Robert Conyers."

"Robert Conyers?"

"Yeah, you and I grew up in the neighborhood knowing him as Blinky," Jonathan said.

"The hell you say!" Henderson blurted out. Even Matthews, who had just known Blinky for being a blind beggar from his rides uptown, was surprised.

"Yes, apparently, it's been a gift he's had for years, since childhood, I think. It's a long story, and I don't really have the time to talk about it, but hopefully, he'll be able to see it for our sake. If it knows it's visible, it might stay hidden long enough for us to place the idol in quarantine so shamans coming from Brazil tomorrow can take it back."

"What shamans?"

"Oh, sorry, I didn't tell you about that?" Jonathan tried to slip in.

Together, both Henderson and Matthews howled, "No, you didn't!"

"Well, we were able to get the Catholic Church involved, and they're helping us in the transport of the idol back to Brazil."

"Who are we?" Henderson asked.

"Err, right now, I'd rather keep that to myself."

"You've been a busy beaver, haven't you Hood?" Henderson added.

"And thirdly," Jonathan didn't answer him, he just moved on, "All those coming? Have them go by the church down on the avenue and have the Father bless them with Holy Water."

Henderson and Matthews stared at him in virtual disbelief.

At this point, Jonathan couldn't give a shit. He told them, "You go take care of that, and I'll go get Blinky and meet you over at the Sierra's Antique Shop." He checked the time and headed out the door.

Chapter 13

In a warehouse in the Soundview area of the Bronx, Ajax, a "counter" for some drug runners, was staking 500 dollars' worth of twenties and rubber banding them into stacks on a table. A few tables down, others counted and placed small plastic bags of cocaine into larger containers for shipping. There was loud music hip-hopping from a distant corner as a cold breeze would tear through the place every time someone buzzed in.

The cell phone next to Ajax began ringing. He looked at the name shown on the screen. It read Snake.

"Hey Samuels, what's up?" said Ajax.

"Who's this?"

"Ajax."

"Let me speak to Syd."

"What? Can't give me a warm hello?" Ajax laughed.

"Just let me speak to Syd." Samuels insisted.

Ajax said, "Okay, just a minute," and he muted the phone.

"Hey Syd?" he yelled across the warehouse floor, "It's that scum bag, Samuels."

Syd Barnes, a light-skinned, lanky-looking man with a small frame, wearing tailored jeans and a warm sweater with shades hiding scars on his face and accenting a thin mustache, came over to take the phone from Ajax.

"Samuels, what's brewing?" he asked.

"I know where J. Hood will be this afternoon if you're still interested in taking him out."

"Of course, I'm still interested, but the last info you gave me didn't work out too well for my boys," Syd reminded Samuels.

"That's because your boys started talking before they started shooting."

"Not according to Jacob 'Deep Blade' Williams, they ran up on Hood and must've spooked him, and still he handled himself pretty good for being off the force so long. Maybe you should've just given us his address."

"Nah, that would've been too obvious, needed it to look like a street mugging, and anyway fuck that loser; I thought I made it easy for you, I had someone in the neighborhood watching his ass, let's just hope Jacob doesn't talk," Samuels said.

"Deep Blade won't talk, don't lose any sleep over him. I'd like to know why you couldn't tell me about Hood earlier when I called you?

"My partner and I were working a crime scene. It's like I told you earlier; Hood didn't fit into it until now. Okay?"

"Yeah, okay, so where and when is this next so-called opportunity?" Syd asked.

"It's supposed to take place later this afternoon, he'll be at Sierra's Antiques on the corner of 56th Street and 1st Avenue, and as a bonus, Captain Henderson will be there," Samuels teased. The 59th Street Bridge is an excellent place to chill until you take them out.

"Hmm, I've always been one for dessert. I'll show up myself just to make sure things are handled right."

"Maybe you should. I'm sure Jonathan would love to see you again."

"Yeah, and just before he'd close his eyes for the last time, I'll tell him it was you who placed the explosive device in his car that killed his wife."

"Just make sure he's near-death first, and don't let your goons go off shooting me."

"Now, why would I have them go doing that?" Syd snickered.

"I just know you can be a little expansive in your thinking, but I still got Hood's report and evidence I lifted from the Captain's desk, and if something should happen to me, well I don't have to paint a picture, do I?"

"Okay, we'll wait outside and hit you as you guys come out of the shop, so be the last one to come out and live or walk in front and be the first to die. You write your ending." Syd offered his solution.

"Gotcha," and just as he ended his conversation, Jonathan walked through the bathroom door and startled the hell out of him, to the point where he stumbled with his phone causing it to tumble to the floor and slide across over the tile, stopping at Jonathan's feet. Jonathan picked it up just as the screen went dark. Samuels didn't know if he saw the initials S.B. on the phone or not. He wasn't sure, and Jonathan wasn't really in the mood to chat with him after the volley of racist shit he blurted out earlier. He didn't even exchange a glance. Jonathan just picked up the phone and said to Samuels, "Not a good time to get clumsy; it could get you killed. I'm going to pick up Blinky. Head into Henderson's office; he'll explain everything."

Jonathan took a pissed, washed his hands, took one look at Samuels, and left.

Samuels mumbled an apology so low that Jonathan couldn't have heard it. He was unable to read Jonathan's face when he left. *What did he mean by "it could get you killed?" Did Jonathan see the screen? Would he even know what S.B. means if he did see?*

He started washing his hands, especially the side with the scratch from the woman back at the apartment he and Matthews went to; it was beginning to irritate him. He peered at his reflection in the mirror, popped a few pills to try and relax, and then started yelling at himself, "Stop it! Stop this shit, mother fucker! You're thinking to Goddamn much, take it to the end. Let's finish this!"

Another officer came in and heard him shouting; he just shook his head and walked into a stall. Samuels tried to straighten up and offer a faint smile and chuckle to give the impression that everything was alright. He figured it was time to get the hell out of there and go back into the captain's office and maybe get a band-aid along the way.

Meanwhile, Syd Barnes got together with a number of his crew. They made preparations for his escapade later on in the day.

Jonathan had given Blinky a ring to let him know he was coming to pick him up; he gave him a rundown that it was Carlos who had picked up the idol. The plan was to go to Mr. Sierra's place of business and arrest Carlos, and he needed Blinky to keep an eye out for the creature in case it showed up. Blinky agreed to wait for him.

On the drive up, Jonathan felt uneasy. He wasn't the kind of person to reveal so much in such a short length of time. Jonathan felt like he emptied himself and left himself open to a bunch of strangers, strangers who were not prone to listen to or accept his views even though he knew them professionally. But as far as this matter went, they were strangers, and he was still playing this by ear, or gut, and to be honest with himself, he didn't know if anything he had suggested would solve anything.

And then there was Samuels, Jonathan was able to understand the disrespectful slant on views, where opinions that were out of place to the situation would be blurted out, but Samuels was virtually tight lip with his shit; something didn't quite feel right in the way he was behaving.

As he pulled up in the car, he called out to Blinky and got out to help him into the car. He then called up Matthews to let him and Henderson know they were on their way to the Antique shop. Matthews told him that Henderson had assigned two officers with hazmat suits to handle the idol, along with a special van.

"Sounds good," Jonathan told him, "Be there around 5:30, before closing?"

"Okay, we're all set."

Syd Barnes sat at a table with four of his associates around him, "We'll get there early, but the plan is to open fire on them as they come out of the shop and not before. It should be getting dark by the time things go down. I want Hood taken out, along with Henderson if possible. Got it?

163

They all nodded and got up to walk through their warehouse, leaving others to package the cocaine, two cars were waiting outside, and they opened the doors, one or two of them taking a hit of cocaine from a tassel mini spoon, causing the rest of them to burst out in hysterics. They climbed in, and the cars headed off in the direction of Manhattan.

Henderson stood outside the steps of the precinct with Matthews and Samuels, along with six other officers. Two of them just came back from the church on the avenue. They brought a priest with them to pray and anoint them with Holy Water. Some of them thought it was strange, to say the least when the Father told them to get closer, repeat the Lord's prayer, and ask for protection for what they were about to face. They did as they were told, not wanting to upset their captain. Only Samuels eased away from the group. The last thing he wanted was to be touched by Holy Water. The move caught Matthews' eye, but he just presumed it was some of the dislikes Samuels held for Jonathan.

After the Father blessed them, he turned to go back to the church. Henderson thanked him and turned to his men, "I don't want any sirens on. I don't want to let Carlos Sierra, our prime suspect, know we're coming. Only officers Simms and Mallory, with the hazmat suits, are to handle the artifact in question. Is that understood?"

"Yes, sir," they all responded.

"Okay," said Henderson.

They all climbed into their vehicles and pulled off.

Chapter 14

"So, how do you feel about this?" Jonathan asked Blinky as they neared their destination.

'Wow, so this is downtown? I haven't been here in a while," said Blinky.

"What, too crowded for you?"

"Oh yeah, it's crowded, more than you think." Blinky sat back in his seat and closed his eyes,

Jonathan pulled over at a corner and went to the trunk of his car. And pulled out an item. He came around on Blinky's side, opened the door, and handed him the piece.

"Put this on." He told Blinky.

"What is it?"

"It's something from my earlier days, a bullet-proof vest."

"What? I don't want —"

"Don't argue; wear it under your coat." He helped Blinky with his coat off and adjusted the vest, saying, "I remember what Joey said this morning, and things might not go the way I planned, so please do what I say."

"Okay, but what about you?"

"Well, at least I'm strapped," Jonathan sighed, "And besides, if anything gets crazy, I can always hide behind the blind guy."

They both burst into laughter as Jonathan got back in and drove to the site.

When Jonathan pulled up, he could see police vehicles about a block away from Sierra's business. Henderson had a few extra officers directing the flow of traffic. Some blocks north of Henderson's patrol, Barnes' crew stayed quiet in their cars. They waited for the cops to make their move.

Jonathan saw Henderson directing him to pull in.

"Hmm, gets dark quick around here," said Jonathan getting out of his car and going around to take Blinky out.

"Yeah," Henderson said, "and being cloudy doesn't help either."

Henderson leaned forward to take Blinky's hand, "Blinky, it's been years. I'm sorry to have to meet under these circumstances."

Blinky was very blunt with Henderson, "Hello Mark, I already know you're not sorry, but it's all good."

Henderson was taken aback a little; Jonathan just shrugged his shoulder while raising his eyebrows as if to say, "Hey, it's Blinky." Jonathan said, "Henderson, let's make sure the idol's somewhere in the shop before your boys in the hazmat suits come in."

Henderson drew his men closer and told them to drive their vehicles right up to the corner to block anyone from running out, and he told the officers in the hazmat suits to wait until he called them. He told Jonathan to stay close to Blinky and walk him in after entering. Samuels remained by the car when the captain called them to meet. For some unknown reason, he wanted to avoid being seen by Blinky.

"Let's do this," Henderson said.

Three police cars pulled up close and covered

the corner as everyone exited their vehicle. Jonathan and Blinky walked the short distance and were a few seconds behind them when Henderson and his crew filed into the shop, causing the bell over the entrance door to continue to chime.

The shop was open, but no one seemed to be there. Henderson called out, "Mr. Sierra, Mr. Francisco Sierra. Is Carlos Sierra here with you? We are the New York City Police with a warrant to search your premises and arrest your son Carlos. Please respond." He called out again, "Mr. Francisco Sierra."

There was no response. Henderson took out his weapon and turned to instruct his men to spread out but be silent about it. He then looked at Jonathan, who was watching Blinky for any sign of anything unusual. Jonathan looked back at Henderson and whispered, "Nothing yet."

Then a sound of books falling from a height in a backroom startled them all as they inched closer to the door from where it came.

Matthews was off to one side of Henderson, and he took a quick look back to see where his partner was. Samuels had his gun out like everyone else, but he had a curious smile on his face. Another sound from the room drew his attention away from Samuels.

There was an ornate antique lamp on a beautifully wood-crafted desk and behind it in the corner of the room laid the bloody and shredded body of Mr. Francisco Sierra. He was dead and held in the blood-soaked, slashed arms of Carlos Sierra, who was weeping while talking to his deceased father, totally unaware of the officers who had filed into the room and stood there surrounding him.

167

* * *

"Papa, you are such a weak man, afraid to take advantage of the things that life has brought you. When you told me about the creature in the mirror and the possible power behind the idol that Mr. Angler had you look at, I knew I, your son Carlos saw the connection between the creature and the totem. I followed Mr. Angler on a binge, drinking with Mr. Simmons' wife, and walked by close enough to hear him say he wished that she wasn't married. He sent the creature after him just by thinking it, and when he heard about Simmons' death, he wanted all traces of his connection gone, again the being started killing everyone connected.

"But I saved you Papa, me, your no-good son Carlos. I was able to steal the idol from Angler. Daniel and I did it. We figured out how to control it too. It's a great and powerful gift that was given to us to use as our protector, and we brought it here. Papa, aren't you proud of me? You don't have to be afraid anymore. It won't harm you. You hear me, Papa?" He screamed, beating on the mangled flesh of this father's corpse before he slumped over and died beside him.

Henderson stood there, shocked like the rest of them, "They, literally tore each other to pieces. Look at all the symbols."

Blinky squeezed Jonathan's hand, "One of them had the creature in them, the other one's infected with the virus. I think someone sent the creature after both of them. It must have been jumping from one to the other as they ripped themselves to shreds." He said.

"It's here! It's here!" came a voice from the back of the room. They all turn to see it was Samuels violently shaking, enough to have his gun fall from him, while he scratched at the now swollen wound on his hand. "It's here. I can feel it."

Blinky turned and yelled, "Don't touch him! He's infected with the virus." He could feel some unknown energy that seemed to be consuming his aura.

Matthews saw him scratching his hand, "That damn Daniels woman scratched him at her apartment." Considering Samuels' strange behavior, he was pissed with himself for not picking up on it sooner.

"What do we do?" Jonathan asked, directing his question to Blinky.

"Just wait a sec," Blinky said. "Give him some room." And to Henderson, "No one should touch the blood on those bodies; it's worse than we thought."

The other officers backed away. Blinky took a bag out of his pocket and tore it open, pulling some sage. He gave it to Jonathan and told him not to light it just yet.

"I hear you; I'm coming." Samuels was calling to something. He turned around and slowly went out of the room, and headed toward a basement door that was ajar. "I'm coming."

"Officers, wait!" Blinky said, "Jonathan, light the sage."

"Got it," Jonathan said.

"Now blow the smoke on each person in the room before they follow him down. I hope you got your Holy-Water-spray mixture on you." Blinky said.

"Wouldn't leave home without it," Jonathan whispered nervously to Blinky as he blew the sage smoke on the other officers, himself, and Blinky.

Henderson called the officers in the hazmat suits and told them that the idol was at this location and for them to make their approach and that to head for the basement area. He asked them to call for another group of officers in hazmat gear, as there were bodies in the shop.

Matthews was shaken by seeing his partner in the state he was in; he knew Samuels had his flaws, but then again, who didn't, and seeing him like this bothered him. He made a solid effort to pull himself together.

Matthews and Henderson cautiously lead the group of officers down the steps to the basement. They were all feeling a little hyper, but somehow the smell of the sage on their clothing had a soothing effect on them. Jonathan replaced his revolver in his holster and took out his small spray bottle, and placed the burning sage in his other hand. Blinky took out a pouch of his own and held onto it as Jonathan and another officer helped him down the basement stairs

The basement ran the full length of the store, there was a loose hanging light bulb dangling from a wood studded ceiling further down from them. They could see the shadowy silhouette of Samuels standing a few yards away from a three-foot carved wooden piece leaning against the wall in a far corner of the basement.

When they circled Samuels, they could see a tall young black man rocking his head back and forth in the corner. A few partially eaten, giant, dead rats were on the floor beside him. His clothes were in rags.

"It's Daniel, Carlos's close friend. What the fuck?" Jonathan grimaced in disgust.

"He's infected, in a bad way and that's the artifact you're looking for," Blinky told him.

Daniels looked at them, squatting down next to the idol piece. He began to snicker at them.

"Can't you hear it? I can, I can understand it. It talks to me in a way you could never understand. Carlos just wanted to save his 'Papa,' his dear, sweet Papa, but it just wanted to go home. He tried to use it to hurt people, to make it his pet." He quietly giggled at the idea. "I had to save it from Carlos and those who knew about it, for only I can save it. I told it I would find its home and take it back. Yeah, I showed Carlos and his father. Carlos didn't believe me, now he knows. Yeah, now he knows. Yeah, Like you'll all know!"

Daniel lovingly stroked the idol, "And now you want to take it from me? NO!" He screamed.

"Jonathan, it's here!" Blinky yelled.

Suddenly everyone could hear the piled-up furniture being splintered and turned over as if some massive creature was rummaging through the place, heading in their direction, but no one could see it except Blinky.

"It's going toward Daniel!" Blinky yelled.

Jonathan started blowing large puffs of the still-burning sage toward Daniel.

"It's slowing it down, but . . ." Blinky observed.

Daniel quickly rose up off his feet; he held a large cleaver in his hand, lunging forward and deeply slicing the officer's arm nearest him. Daniel let out a harrowing, unworldly scream as he charged Matthews and Henderson. The officers fired over eight shots into him, and he slowly collapsed with a bizarre look in his eyes, going down with the cleaver raised and shattering the one over-hanging light bulb.

All hell broke loose as some police scurried for cover in the dark; shots were fired randomly during the mayhem.

"Hold your fire, damn it!" screamed Henderson, who, like others, was trying to adjust his eyes to the darkness when other officers quickly turned on their flashlights.

Blinky could see it rise out from Daniel's corpse and try to enter another person in the room, but it couldn't. Somehow the sage smoke that filled the room was causing it to move more slowly than it could. He figured out the next available target and yelled to Jonathan, "It's working its way to Samuels

Every flashlight shown on the spot where Samuels was left standing, he wasn't there. The flashlights frantically searched for him, finding him by the wall. As they lit up Samuels' figure, Jonathan virtually soaked him a spray of Holy Water. Samuels began to scream as the holy acid rained on him, but Jonathan kept on spraying, with Samuels trying to wipe it clear from the skin on his face and his eyes as he cowered back against the wall.

The creature turned again. Somehow it knew that it was visible to Blinky, and it needed to stop him from seeing it. It started moving toward him and roared against the dislike of the sage smoke. It became partly visible to everyone in the room; it was hideous, becoming even more noticeable as it near Blinky. Blinky threw down his pouch to have it explode with a potpourri of special scented herbs and fragrances, causing the creature to scream and vanish.

"It's gone," Blinky said, with a sigh of relief that quickly spread throughout the room.

An officer found another light fixture at the other end of the basement and turned it on as the men in the hazmat suits came in to claim the idol.

* * *

Syd Barnes had been checking his watch. He began to wonder what was taking the police so long to come out of the antique shop. He got out of the car, motioning the rest of his crew to do the same and take positions surrounding the entrance, but to remain as casual looking as possible so as not to look suspicious to any pedestrians in the street.

Henderson showed the officers in the hazmat suits the wooden idol, instructing them to avoid Daniel's corpse. There would be another hazmat unit to deal with the bodies. They went over to the artifact and covered it with a protective cloth before placing it in a hexagonal container, while two officers were doing their best to restrain Samuels, who was still suffering from the spray of Holy Water.

Matthews was looking around and saw the package holding the replica of the idol underneath some shattered furniture and told Henderson and Jonathan about it.

"What do you want to do with it?" Matthews asked.

"Like one idol wasn't bad enough," joked Jonathan

As the officers began leaving with the real idol, Samuel started to scream, "Don't take it out there. It'll be hurt." He started fighting with the two officers in earnest, knocking them back and slamming a right cross into the face of a third approaching officer.

"Oh, what the fuck now!" cried Henderson as Samuels started running up the stairs with everyone else in pursuit.

Jonathan gently nudged Blinky along, "Damn, that creature better not be upstairs cause I'm all out of the spray. Shit!"

Upstairs, Samuels was still fighting with an officer who tried to tackle him before he decided to run out the door. Samuels kicked him off and got up to run as two officers reached him before going out of the entrance, pulling him past the officers in the hazmat suits and onto the street. When they fell out the doors, all hell broke loose.

Barnes ordered his men to open fire with the two officers, and Samuels caught in a hail of bullets; they all went down, hitting the pavement hard. Along with Henderson and Jonathan, other officers drew their weapons and went toward the entrance, firing in the area of the gun flashes, not genuinely knowing who was firing at them.

"Stay here!" Jonathan shouted to Blinky and the officers carrying the idol as he got low to the floor and worked his way to the door. He rolled along the ground and was able to get to one of the parked police cars in front of the entrance, where he and a few officers who followed his lead took cover and started firing back.

Pedestrians screamed, running every-which-way to clear the streets. Henderson called for backup while walking to the door, firing. Jonathan looked back and saw him and couldn't believe his stupidity. He lunged again, grabbed Henderson's arm, and yanked him down just as incoming rounds of bullets tore the store's door frame to shreds.

"What the fuck were you thinking, just walking out here like that? Are you out of your Goddamn mind?" Jonathan shouted.

"I just wanted to get a quick look; I think it's Syd Barnes and his crew. That's him over behind the UPS truck," Henderson pointed out to him.

They could hear the windows shatter behind them. Jonathan checked his weapon, not sure how long they could hold out.

"Hey Hood, you dead yet?" It was Barnes yelling from his position.

Jonathan just fired a shot in the direction of the voice.

Syd Barnes briefly stepped to the side to say, "I guess not."

Jonathan had put a bead on him and patiently waited for Barnes to step out. When he did, he fired again. This time Jonathan hit Barnes dead center, he went down.

Barnes' crew started firing with newfound vigor, pissed out of their minds that Barnes went down. Another officer was shot in the hip, while another lay sprawled on his back, moaning. Just then, other officers, along with the hazmat unit that Henderson had called in earlier to get the bodies in the shop, arrived and squeezed Barnes' men between them and Henderson's group as other units showed up from other 911 calls. Barnes' men had nowhere to go and soon surrendered after a number of them went down on the pavement.

Three of Henderson's officers lay dead with two others wounded, one gravely in the aftermath. Barnes and three of his cohorts were killed.

Henderson and Jonathan got up, the worse for wear. They checked the area, looking over to see Matthews and others holstering their weapons. They went over to where Samuels had fallen with the two cops laying on top of him, thinking he was dead as well. They heard a soft moan coming from the pile and moved closer, instructing the EMS, who just had arrived in hazmat suits, to move the bodies of the two officers over to see who was moaning. It was Samuels, wounded but still alive.

EMS asked that everyone get back as they picked him up to put him on a stretcher and placed the two dead officers with him in body bags with warnings on them. As they started to secure Samuels with straps, his hand jutted out, pointing at Jonathan, and he was ranting, "Why, damn it why? Why not you in the car? Why did it have to be Cynthia? You should have died; I meant it for you to die, you bastard!" Then he collapsed, leaving the EMS and everyone else in earshot shocked by the revelation.

Jonathan pulled out his gun, aiming it at Samuels, screaming, "NO!" He was about to pull the trigger, but Matthews and Henderson were able to wrestle it away from him as he collapsed to his knees, whimpering, "No, no, damn you, no."

Henderson motioned to EMS to get Samuels out of here ASAP. Jonathan slowly rose to his feet with Matthews and Henderson, consoling him, as best they could, to see if he was okay. Jonathan looked around at the scene of mayhem with tears in his eyes and painfully nodded that he would be okay.

"We'll look into that statement ASAP," Henderson promised him.

"Hood! Hood! Get in here. It's your friend!" An officer loudly shouted from inside the shop as another officer rushed to the door opening, beaconing for him to hurry inside.

"Blinky?" Fear washed over Jonathan like a tidal wave. In all the commotion, he forgot all about Blinky. His heart raced as he feared the worse. He rushed past the cop and attempted to gain some level of control of his nerves as a situation he in no way could've envisioned began taking place.

He entered the shop and saw an officer pointing down to the floor where two legs showed behind a turned-over, large wooden table that obstructed his view. He rushed closer as an EMS unit followed him in. Blinky was lying on the floor in a puddle of blood. Jonathan gingerly pulled back one side of Blinky's coat to see there was one bullet lodged in the bullet-proof vest he had given Blinky, but he was bleeding from another shot in his shoulder. He was semi-conscious and groaning in pain.

"Blinky! Blinky!" Jonathan called, trying to get him to answer. After a few attempts Blinky painfully, but finally responded with, "So my first ride in your car and the best you can do is to take me to this shootout, shithole!"

Jonathan nervously chuckled and then moved out of the way to allow EMS to attend to Blinky.

"How bad is he?" he asked worriedly.

"It could've been a lot worse; it's a good thing the bullet didn't work its way into his chest. It went straight on through." One of them said to him. Tears came on the cusp of Jonathan's eyelids just thinking the thought of something happening seriously to Blinky, someone with who he was hoping to create a long-term friendship.

After they took Blinky out, other officers and EMS in hazmat suits came in to deal with the bodies of Mr. Sierra, his son, Carlos in the back office, and Daniel downstairs in the basement.

Jonathan came outside to see an overly crowded area with hundreds of people and news crews getting set up beneath the dark sky. He needed a drink, but all Henderson could offer him was a cigarette from a battle-worn, crumpled pack of cigarettes. Jonathan took one, not wanting it, but as a sign of camaraderie over the experience they both shared.

"Samuels, all this time Samuels, damn," Matthews said as he came over to take a bent-up cigarette out of Henderson's pack. He shook his head and looked at Jonathan, "How's your boy, Blinky?"

"Yeah, how is Blinky?" Henderson added in.

"It was a close call, but I think he'll pull through," Jonathan responded, trying to sound hopeful for his own sake.

"That's good to hear," Matthew said.

"Yeah, I'm surprised, and I don't know how he did it, but Blinky came through for us. You can thank him for the whole team. Who would've known that old crazy blind kid would've had that kind of gift?" Henderson mused.

"Yeah, but then again, who would've thought that a guy like Samuels could've involved himself in the death of my wife, Cynthia," Jonathan said, revealing the buildup of tension in his voice.

"I promise you, Hood, I'm going to get to the bottom of this. I'll get a warrant, and we'll go through Samuels' premises with a fine-tooth comb, along with any other places he may have." Henderson swore.

"I'm only wondering how much he was into Syd Barnes' crew and maybe others. What was their connection?" Jonathan continued thinking out loud.

"Yeah, and to think I road with him all these years and didn't know jack shit about him!" Matthews confessed to them.

Their experience together had indeed changed the impression they held for one another. Enough for Henderson to offer Jonathan his hand, "I apologize for any misunderstandings you and I may have had in the past."

"I'll hold you to that," Jonathan said, shaking his hand, "Knowing all too well there'll be misunderstandings in our future."

Matthews and Henderson nodded in quiet laughter mixed with the relief they felt for merely surviving one more day. They knew they "dodged a bullet," where others around them weren't so fortunate.

"One sec, I need to call someone," Jonathan said, stepping over to the side to make a call.

"Hello, this is Joanna speaking," the voice said on the other end.

"Hello Joey, it's me, Jonathan. Blinky, err, I mean Robert's been shot. Yes, they've taken him to Lenox Hill Hospital. They say he should pull through. Joey, Robert was effective and brave in helping us retrieve the idol. Yes, you can let Father Bennett know. Okay, I'll meet you there and explain everything. Okay, bye."

"Joanna?" Henderson asked with that hurt look in his eyes.

"Yeah."

"Well, when you see her, tell her I said hi and let her know I'm sorry about Blinky."

"Sure, no problem. Hey, here comes the camera crew, do what you do best." Jonathan bowed, shook his hand, Matthews' hand, and some of the other fellow officers on the scene, and walked off to get in his ride down the street. He'd leave Captain Henderson to clean it up; it was something he was good at doing. Henderson had surprised him and came through when needed. Who would've thought?

Jonathan looked around him and looked behind him at the flashing lights of the police and emergency vehicles. Stopping when he reached his car, turned around, and just wondered how the hell he ever survived that mess, his mind raced back over of the memories of what he had endured over in the last few days. Opening his car door, Jonathan climbed in and sat there for a few minutes, shaking, his hands trembling. He remembered the look of the creature down in the basement; he wasn't entirely as prepared for it as he thought. Ir might've been a time to act cool, but Jonathan knew better. Then again, maybe that's only a small yet necessary part of it, looking cool when dealing with some of your worst fears. He knew that the creature wasn't dead, just gone for the moment and with no master to give it orders, well maybe. He started the car and took off for Lenox Hill Hospital to meet up with Joey and learn about Blinky.

Jonathan decided to make a quick run to Bellevue Hospital to check on Mr. Angler. It was in his nature to want to wrap things up. He still wasn't clear how Carlos Sierra could secure enough I.D. to impersonate being Mr. Angler's son. Carlos must have found Mr. Angler's address and went to his house to rob him.

Jonathan planned to use his detective-style swagger, taking an old badge from his glove compartment. When he reached Bellevue, Jonathan talked to Dr. Leonard, the doctor Captain Henderson spoke earlier. Hood wanted the doctor to know he was with Henderson, listening to their conversation. Dr. Leonard needed to know that things might get tough for him if he didn't cooperate with the police department.

Dr. Leonard called a nurse attendant over out of concern for his position.

"Nurse Luis Savage, this is Detective Jonathan Hood. Please take him into the ward to see Mr. Angler."

Nurse Savage was a big man, about 6.5', 230 to 250 pounds, with a tough-looking exterior. He stood by Jonathan and brooded while he sorted through his keys. He never said a word, just nodded, and motioned for Jonathan to follow him.

Damn, this guy looks like he should be in a padded cell, with the keys thrown away, Jonathan thought.

As they walked past some rooms down the ward, Jonathan could hear a woman screaming over and over, "He's here, the Master is here!"

Nurse Savage just growled.

When they reached Mr. Angler's door, Nurse Savage grabbed Jonathan's shoulder with his huge hand, turned him around, and showed him two fingers, meaning he had two minutes with Angler; Jonathan noticed an unusually long nail on his pinky finger. The look on Savage's face told him – two minutes, no more. He didn't care if Jonathan was a cop or not. He slid the door panel to the side for Jonathan to view Angler.

Angler was in the corner of his padded cell giggling. When he heard the panel slide open, he turned to look at Jonathan and said, "Did the black-hunter ant find its wooden home? Took it from my son, did you? The black-hunter ant is safe now? No more attacks? Maybe the black- hunter ant thinks he's safe? Hey? Looking for the Master? Could be the Master is looking for you."

Jonathan had enough. He shook his head and closed the panel, turned, and looked at Nurse Savage, who had a maniacal smile on his face. Did he enjoy what Angler said?

What did he mean by mentioning the words "my son?" Did Angler somehow know about Carlos, and were they somehow connected through the virus?

"Maybe it wasn't such a good idea coming up here," he mumbled to himself. He walked off the ward in a rush, with Nurse Savage still standing there smiling at him like a fucking lunatic. Jonathan found his way to Dr. Leonard and just waved as he left the floor as quickly as possible. He got an unsettling feeling from the place and that nurse, Luis Savage. Jonathan would tell Blinky about this experience after Blinky got well. Right now, he needed to be with his friend.

Epilogue

Jonathan arrived at the hospital a short time after Joey. When he saw her, every other concern on his mind vanished. He went and put his arm around her, doing his best to comfort her. They sat on a bench outside in the waiting area nearby the ER, but while she appreciated his efforts, she was well trained as a nurse in the Emergency Room at Harlem Hospital. If anything, it was a long day, and she had to leave work to be with Blinky. Joey only needed Jonathan's shoulder to lean on while they waited for Blinky to come out of surgery.

"I had a feeling something was gonna get crazy today. I mean, I could just feel it!" She said worriedly.

"Yeah, that's why I gave him the vest to wear. In my head, I heard your voice from this morning's conversation, and I'm glad I did. That bullet that lodged in the vest would've probably caused much worse damage." Jonathan confessed.

She sat up and gave him a sharp rap on his shoulder, "What were you thinking bringing a blind man to a crime scene?"

He was lost for words and just looked at her in a way that pleaded for forgiveness.

"Oh, I know it was probably the only thing you could think of at the time." She added, "Men!" There was a tinge of disgust in her voice.

"Honestly, Joey, I don't think anyone could've predicted what went down at that place. What we thought would be an arrest with some basic problems turned into major, all-out chaos. I'd much rather it be me in that surgery room," he offered her.

She could see his eyes beginning to tear and realized the level of his sincerity, "Oh Jonathan, I'm not blaming you, I'm just tired, mad, and, to be honest scared. I'm mean, with all we read, with all we believe, and with all we claim to know, suddenly an aspect of one reality reaches in and turns our reality into shredded trash. We can play at being calm and knowledgeable about it, but we'd be damned if we didn't just want to run somewhere and hide 'til the coast is clear." She squeezed his hand in a loving, comforting way. "Now, since we're waiting, tell me about what happened."

Jonathan was able to calm himself down and told her about his day from the time he left Blinky. He could see the story was bruising her senses at specific points. He talked of Samuels to the bodies of the Sierras, Daniels, and the creature in the basement. Then the shootout with Syd Barnes and some of his gang members out on the avenue to Samuel's confession. When he finished, all she could say was, "Damn!"

After a few coffees and more small talk, the surgeon came out to see them. Joey introduced herself to him as Joanna, a trauma nurse at Harlem Hospital, so he explained medical jargon. She then translated it into everyday English to Jonathan. She shook his hand and thanked him.

"So, how is he?" Jonathan asked.

Her cell phone rang. It was Father Bennett returning

her call. She explained that the idol was indeed retrieved and currently held in a downtown police station in quarantine. And that she would have her friend, Jonathan Hood, the person at the apartment where they met, text him the address and the person or persons with whom he should speak. She then wrote down his info for Jonathan.

Meanwhile, Jonathan had been pacing all the time she was on the phone, "Well, tell me about Blinky."

"Oh," she said smiling, "Good news, the doctor said he lost a lot of blood, but that they were able to stitch him up and that within a few days, he should be able to be back on his corner begging with the best of them."

"No, he …"

"No, I just added that last part. Come on; they're taking him to the tenth floor, and don't forget to text Father Bennett the address and such. You should see your face." She grabbed his arm, laughing with relief, and walked him to the bank of elevators.

When they walked into Blinky's room, a nurse attending him asked them to come back in about half an hour and that he would be responsive by then. They went to the waiting area and waded through some more small talk.

"By the way," Jonathan said, "Henderson told me to tell you hi."

"Oh, really now? And to what do I owe this to?" She offered a sly glance.

"Listen, I don't know if he's going to be the same

'ol asshole that you and I are familiar with, but earlier this evening, he handled himself very well, considering the circumstances."

"We are talking about the same man, aren't we?"

"Yeah, yeah," Jonathan laughed, "Caught a side of him that I never expected was there."

"Well, that side was always there. Henderson was just never fond of showing it."

"Humph."

The nurse came by and told them that their friend was awake.

"Joey, you go first. I'll be in a sec," he said, pulling out his phone, "I need to text Father Bennett the information he needs.

"Ok, see you there." She said as she walked by the nurses' station only to hear one nurse say to another, "That new patient we just admitted sure does blink a lot." Joey couldn't help from giggling to herself as she walked into Robert's room. Still, when she walked into the room and saw him sitting up with all the blood-stained bandages, she was moved to grateful tears that he was just alive. She smiled, wiping the tears away, and repeatedly kissed him.

They were pretty talkative when Jonathan showed up, doing his best to smile. Joey told Blinky that she would be outside and, as she passed Jonathan, hinted to him to keep it short so that Blinky could rest, but before she left, she heard Blinky say, "Jonathan, you've changed, your aura's different." She decided to stay by the door and listen.

"Oh sure, now you're gonna use your injury to tell me I'm the one who's changed, buddy; you better take a good look in the mirror." Jonathan leaned over to give him a gentle hug, "Glad to see that you're still with us."

"No, I'm serious; there's definitely a change in your aura. It's brighter than it's been, and there seems to be an access point or portal showing on your right and along the edges of your aura where I can glimpse other beings."

"What? I hope it isn't anything like that creature again," he joked half-heartedly, trying to put that stuff behind him.

"No, no, they're more like allies or guides," Blinky insisted.

"Well, while I can use all the help I can get, how are you doing?" he had his fill of this spiritual stuff today and wanted to skirt the issue. "Oh, and here are your shades. You left them on the floor in the shop. Put them on; you're scaring the nurses."

"I could be better, I supposed, and thanks," Blinky said, taking the hint to leave the aura topic alone. "Oh yeah, a lot better."

Joey took what Blinky said about Jonathan's aura and began dwelling on its meaning as she turned down the hall to make arrangements for room and board at a nearby hotel.

Jonathan talked with Blinky about what they had gone through with Henderson and Matthews. He also dealt with Samuels' confession about killing his wife, Cynthia.

Blinky got quiet, going over thoughts and memories of Samuels. "I'm sorry I didn't see any connection with him and your wife. While he walked with shadows around him, I thought it was his natural dislike for us and the negative energy he always carried with him. Lord knows he did his best to keep from showing."

"It's nothing I don't' think that even you could've seen. Samuels had us all fooled," Jonathan confessed.

He ended his story with Henderson's apology and thanks for Blinky's help. Jonathan told him to get some healing time. Jonathan was going home to get some much-needed rest as well.

He ran into Joey, who was coming back to sit with Robert; he asked her if she needed a ride back uptown, but she told him she would be staying at a hotel in the neighborhood so that she could check on Robert in the morning.

"So, a brighter aura, eh?" Joey asked.

"Too much medication," Jonathan joked, again trying his best to dance around the topic.

"Humph, oh, Father Bennett texted me. He claims he wants to see us tomorrow when he picks up the idol. I'll call you in the morning," Joey told him.

"And here I thought I was gonna get to sleep in for the day. Okay, see you tomorrow. They kissed each other's cheek, and he left.

When he got home, Jonathan watched the late-night news only to see a report of the shootout in upper mid-Manhattan with videos of Matthews, Henderson, and himself. His first impulse was to watch the interview with Henderson for once, but then he reached over to grab the digital controls deciding he wanted to turn the television off. Henderson's face came on the screen when the reporter asked why the police were in the antique shop, so Jonathan just paused to hear Henderson's answer.

Henderson took his usual stance in front of the camera and began his bullshit. "We had information that a Daniel Jacobs, known as Dealer Dan for the notorious Syd Barnes cartel was here holding the owner, a Mr. Francisco Sierra and his son Carlos hostage over a shipment of cocaine found in certain pieces of furniture. We arrived only to find Mr. Sierra and his son already murdered and the suspect in the basement. The situation turned ugly when the notorious Syd Barnes and his crew arrived to support one of their members, leading to the shootout."

"And the reason for the men in hazmat suits?" The reporter questioned.

"We discovered, via an informant, that the cocaine seized here was highly toxic due to a base chemical used in manufacturing it. As always, we honor the lives of those officers who made the ultimate sacrifice in keeping New York's streets safe from drugs, particularly this deadly drug that would have caused many deaths, and for taking a high-profile criminal off the street. We are indeed blessed to have such fine men and women in our department."

"Eh, Captain Henderson ..." Jonathan turned it off, "Go 'head with your top-of-the-line bullshit Capt. You bad!" he said, chuckling at the sheer speed to which Henderson could paint a black horse white.

He sat on the edge of his bed, tired as hell. There was no glamour, no high fives, nothing to brag about today and today's achievements. Tears came to his eyes, in his tired state, as he realized just how lucky he was to be alive. "Thank you, Cindy, thanks for being with me, and of course, thank you, God."

He leaned back on his pillow and whispered things to his Cindy. If anyone could understand him, she could. He talked lovingly to her until he fell asleep.

He was surprised to receive an early-morning call from Henderson asking for him to head down to the precinct at 2 pm. There, the return of the idol piece would take place; in a semi-formal presentation on the steps of the precinct with the U.S, Customs officials, Brazilian Customs officials, Father Bennett, some shamans from the Brazil basin, and some other notorieties.

Jonathan got up, feeling better and glad to know that the idol was on its way home. He took a quick shave, spruced up, and headed on down to get some breakfast. Turning the corner to walk down the avenue, Jonathan noticed Blinky's space on the corner by the bar was empty. A strange shudder came over him. He made a note to himself to visit him tomorrow, for Blinky needed to relax today. After breakfast, he sat in the Silver Bullet for a while, read the Daily News, and headed downtown.

When he arrived, he parked in the police parking lot and walked around to the front where about twenty to thirty folding chairs sat, a podium with microphones and people gathering, photographers amongst them. He saw Matthews mingling about and waved.

"What the hell? I thought this was going to be a 'here it is, thanks, see you later' affair." He said to himself, seeing Joey taking a seat in the back row.

He went over and sat next to her, placing a kiss on her cheek, "Did you know about this?"

She laughed, "Jonathan, it's Mark Henderson, this is what he does, this is what he's all about. Someone left a message at the hospital. You can't expect him to change overnight, can you now?"

"Yeah, I guess not. I caught a piece of Henderson's crap dished out on the news; it looks like he's back in the saddle, if not the limelight. So, how's Blinky?"

She gave him an ok nod.

They sat and watched as the seats quickly filled up, and then the ceremony began. There the typical country-to-country political orations were made. Father Bennett and Captain Henderson shared the podium, complimented each other, and invited the Brazilian shamans and their translator to accept the box with the incased idol. Camerapersons took pictures, with small state gifts exchanged, but no mention of Jonathan's participation or assistance.

Joey noticed it also, "Yeah, Mark is back."

Jonathan just waved it off, and when the presentation was over, he stood to go.

Joey stood up and grabbed his hand, "He's not getting away with this!" she shouted to him.

"It's okay; really, Joey, it's okay," Jonathan said.

"Oh no," she pulled him reluctantly to where Father Bennett and the Brazilian group stood, saying their goodbyes to Capt. Henderson.

She came in between them and gave Mark Henderson such a stern look. He just stepped back. "Father Bennett."

"Joanna, why I'm so glad you came, good to see you. How are you?"

"Father Bennett, will you please tell the Brazilian translator that this is the man who retrieved the idol and the one who deserves their thanks." She shoved Jonathan in front of her, and then she turned, put her arm around Henderson's, and proceeded to take him off to the side and give him a piece of her mind.

Father Bennett told the translator about Jonathan and introduced him to the two shamans, but they already looked stunned in Jonathan's presence. They reverently bowed their heads and called him a phrase that even the translator had difficulty interpreting. After several attempts, she finally turned to Jonathan and said, "They give you the sovereign title of Hunter!" She turned back to them. Jonathan just stood there, as much grateful as Father Bennett was surprised. Joey and Henderson, who caught the tail end of it, were also shocked. Not particularly familiar with the proper way of saying thank you to them, Jonathan just bowed his head.

The translator turned to the shamans and asked them why they would say that. Then turning to Jonathan, she said, "They said that they could sense that you must have fought well with the creature. It has returned and now attached itself to the idol, and upon their return, it will be released back through the portal."

Jonathan smiled and nodded in thanks, thinking to himself, that's all I wanted to hear, the creature will be going home.

Feeling the slight discomfort in the air, Father Bennett broke the mood and invited all of them to come by the church for brunch.

At the brunch, Joey made small talk with Father Bennett. He told her what he had learned from the Brazilian delegation; that while the Church would keep this incident from the public record, It would note that the shamans told them that other beings and creatures had found their way through the portal since its opening. They informed the Church that once they reseal the portal, those entities may be exiled on our plane of existence until they find another outlet to their home realm.

Joey worked her way over to the table of the Brazilian dignitaries, where both shamans greeted her as one like themselves.

Jonathan was feeling tired after eating his fill and working his way through the crowd. He chattered with Matthews, who told him how Samuels was doing. Matthews said they had found the evidence that Jonathan had given Henderson on Syd Barnes in a personal safe at Samuels' apartment. And that he wasn't as crazy as the others affected by the virus, he would survive his wounds from the shootout, going to trial for Cynthia's death, his connection to the drug cartel, and his involvement with the Barnes' investigation. Jonathan thanked him for all he had done over the past few days.

Jonathan saw Captain Henderson on his way to the door but just waved. He didn't want to hear anything more out of his mouth, not today anyway.

Joey left the table and told the translator to thank the shamans for taking the idol home. One shaman asked their interpreter again, "What did you say to the man who fought the beast?"

"I told him that you said he was a Hunter."

"No, that is not the meaning of the name we gave him." He appeared somewhat worried, if not disappointed.

"I'm sorry, I did my best. Please tell me again; maybe I can still tell him." She apologized

The shaman took his time explaining it, making sure she understood, and had her repeat it to them.

She repeated until they both nodded, "It means Hunter of Spirits, Lost Souls, but from other worlds and that they will come to know you for who you are, for they are drawn to you, as you will be drawn to them." When they were satisfied, she left them to find Jonathan, but he was nowhere to be found for all her looking around.

Jonathan was outside, getting ready to leave and saying goodbye to Joey. Joey asked him, "So are you going to call Gloria?"

"Gloria? Oh, Gloria. Listen, I still haven't figured out how I was drawn to Samantha. I need some time to think about it." He said.

"Take your time. You want me to tell Blinky about your new 'given' title?"

"For what, so he can laugh his ass off next time he sees me?"

"Sure, Hunter sounds cool," she said.

"Alright, go ahead if it will make him feel any better." He kissed her wickedly smiling cheeks and told her he'd see Blinky tomorrow. She walked into a waiting cab and headed across town to see her man.

* * *

It was dark when he pulled up on Bradhurst Ave. He sat in his car and pulled out a cigar before exiting his vehicle; it was time for a smoke. The air had a chill in it while a wistful breeze brushed back and forth, swirling about him. He started his conversation with Cindy with, "Finally! Did you hear that crap about me being a, oh never mind? How have you been today, baby? Don't mind me. I need a victory cigar, yeah, yeah, I'm cutting it in half."

He stopped, dropped half of the cigar, lit his half, and enjoyed the aroma, feeling that he had finally done something worthwhile. When he was about a block away, a shadowy figure appeared behind him wearing a dark coat. It stood over the tossed piece of the cigar. Its face was in shadow beneath a wide brim hat. A hand with a long-wicked pinky nail reached down, picked up the cigar, brought it to its face as a flame came from the long fingernail, and lit it with its touch. The glow of the cigar revealed an unworldly face with red, glowing eyes. It watched Jonathan walk on and turn the corner as the creepy, maniacal smile of Luis Savage sneered in the glow of the hot cigar ashes.

About the Author

Amurá Oñaā, another soul with stories to tell.

www.ingramcontent.com/pod-product-compliance
Lightning Source LLC
Chambersburg PA
CBHW070843120626
46556CB00002B/862